STERLING

STERLING

by Robert Cameron

FIRESTEP
Press

FireStep Publishing
Gemini House
136-140 Old Shoreham Road
Brighton
BN3 7BD

www.firesteppublishing.com

First published by FireStep Press, an imprint
of FireStep Publishing in 2013

ISBN 978-1-908487-13-1
© Robert Cameron, 2013

A CIP catalogue reference for this book is available in the British Library.

Designed by FireStep Publishing
Cover by Ryan Gearing
Typeset by Graham Hales, Derby

Contents

For Aga

Because without her
Robert Cameron would not be here

Acknowledgements

I have had the pleasure of working alongside some of the world's best, most of whom would not appreciate their names being made public. They don't do it for praise but to them my thanks, they know who they are.

I'd also like to acknowledge the hard work of the front line ambulance staff; keep up the good work.

A big thank you to Ryan Gearing for having the courage to take this on and the people at FireStep for putting it together.

Also to Christine Howe for her way with words.

Most of all Mum, Dad, Cath, Alan and Luke. The best family I could ask for.

Loosely based on real events.

Chapter 1

It had felt like a long day in the English Lake District. Even though at that time of year the days were short, it seemed to have dragged. Cam had been unable to sleep; perhaps it was the sunlight keeping him awake – or maybe he knew his past was about to catch up with him. Whatever the reason, as he lay there that night in the darkness of the rest-room, he was tired. Outside the wind had started to pick up, rustling the trees and almost drowning out the sound of the river. The air-pressure had changed and Cam could feel the black clouds rolling in over the hills, bringing rain.

He kept a wary eye on Nick, his crew-mate for the night. Cam was still unsure if it was the done thing to sleep whilst on shift, but if Nick was sleeping he could too. As it happened they had not been out that night. Cam always thought that that if nobody called for an ambulance, all was good in the world. Making one last check he peeked over at Nick – 'still asleep,' Cam thought. It was safe to close his eyes once again and grab another ten minutes' sleep.

The dull hum of the radio beside him woke him from his light sleep. He rolled off the cold fake-leather sofa that had been his makeshift bed on and off for the last year. Now denied the sleep he needed, he grabbed the vibrating handset and squeezed the 'acknowledge' key, accepting the call and silencing the radio.

He stumbled sleepily toward the vehicle bay. By the time he had reached the large door of the garage his balance was restored. Still functioning like an automaton, he pressed the green 'open' button. The motor whirred into action, raising the door and letting in a blast of winter air. The icy current rolled under the opening door and wrapped itself around Cam's legs. 'Christ that's cold,' he thought.

Cam shook himself awake and climbed into the driving seat, noticing the time on the dashboard. It was 03:35.

'My turn to drive again,' he mumbled to himself, pulling forward out of the garage. In the rear-view mirror he could see movement. His colleague closed the garage door behind the ambulance and the light in the garage slowly disappeared. The warm safety of the station already seemed a long way off when the passenger door opened and Nick climbed in.

'Where we going, then?' said Nick.

'Ambleside,' Cam croaked. He looked down at the screen where the details of the call were displayed. 'Fifty-two-year-old male, difficulty breathing.' The moment he finished speaking, the night around the ambulance was lit up with random blue lights. Cam checked left and right, pulled out on to the road and they were off.

'Thought I'd hold back on the sirens and let the public sleep,' Cam said, accelerating out of the village.

'Nice of you,' Nick replied, without looking away from the paper work. 'Thank God the roads are empty,' Cam thought, pushing the ambulance faster and faster towards the address on the screen. He had been lucky so far. He hadn't been to any calls that had been too distressing. That's why he chose to work for the ambulance service in a sleepy part of the Lake District. He'd seen enough.

Normally chatty on route, the crew sat quietly contemplating what might be waiting for them at the end of their journey. Cam's mind wandered as the ambulance rattled down the road. He relished the prospect of his approaching days off, nearly five days in a row – almost unheard of. He would need every one of them for what he had planned.

Suddenly, back to reality, they arrived in Ambleside. A series of sharp left and right turns led them towards the address, and as they drew closer they tried to figure out which side of the street the house would be on.

'Odd numbers on the left,' Nick said, and with that, on came the left spotlight illuminating Nick's side of the street.

'Here, the one with the light on.' Cam pulled over and killed the lights. The crew jumped out of the vehicle. Nick grabbed the response bag and strode swiftly up to the door. Cam was always glad he had been partnered up with Nick; he was one of the area's paramedics that still had some urgency about all calls, a professional approach with which he could identify.

Cam grabbed the oxygen and drugs-bag from the side compartment of the ambulance. Even Cam's limited experience with the service had prepared him to expect anything. The house was warm, a welcome relief from the chill of the early Cumbrian morning. Following the muffled voices from a distant bedroom, Cam made his way down the corridor, looking around and taking in his surroundings. He had learned you could tell so much about the patient from the state of their house. 'Not too bad,' he thought. It was much better than some of the crapholes he had been in.

Halfway through his questioning, Nick knew exactly what was wrong with the patient, and as Cam appeared in the doorway it was clear to him too. The scene was a common one. A male, looking much older than he was, sat up in bed struggling to catch his breath, red-faced and wheezing on inhalation. Looking down at the SP02 monitor that Nick had already put in place, Cam could see that the man's pulse was slightly fast but nothing to worry about, and he had 100% oxygen circulating in his bloodstream. Nick was trying to calm the man using all the usual lines while coaching him to relax his breathing.

Kneeling next to the bed, Cam took the red-faced man's wrist and felt for a pulse, for no other reason than to make the patient feel better. He knew that people were reassured by a medical professional doing something they could recognise.

'Do you have any pins and needles in your fingers at all?' Cam said, with his well-rehearsed caring voice.

'Yes, yes,' gasped the man. Both Nick and Cam knew that this was nothing more than an anxiety attack, more commonly known as a panic attack. 'What the hell could he have to panic about?' wondered Cam. Nothing terrifying ever happened in Ambleside. 'How could he know how it was to be truly terrified?'

While Nick explained to the man in his genuine, caring way that he was going to be OK, Cam glanced around the room, spotting some medication on the cluttered bedside table. He took a closer look. Two types of antidepressant – not a surprise. Doctors seemed to hand those things out like Smarties. Putting the medication boxes next to Nick so he could see them, he began to tidy up the equipment. 'Another life saved,' Cam joked to himself.

Chapter 2

Arriving back at the station always felt good, especially on cold nights like that one. The station was small and tucked away out of view, and had only one crew on at any one time – this suited Cam perfectly. With less than an hour to go before the day-crew would arrive for handover, there was no point in trying to go back to sleep. A few minutes grabbed here and there usually made Cam feel worse. A cup of coffee was a much better idea.

Both members of the weary night-crew sat in the rest-room, the television on in the background. 'Daytime TV – nothing worse,' thought Cam. He waited patiently for the moment that Nick would leave the room so he could flick over to the news. It would not be long; Nick always had something to do in the office.

Once alone, Cam picked up the remote and changed channels. 'Expense scandals! Typical. Put something interesting on – something I can use,' thought Cam. 'This is the only chance I get to watch the news, to gather intelligence.' Scrolling along the bottom of the screen was some breaking news. 'BOMB FOUND IN PRINTER CARTRIDGE ON CARGO AIRCRAFT TIMED TO EXPLODE

OVER THE EASTERN STATES OF THE USA.' 'Interesting, but nothing to do with me any more.' Cam's mind drifted back to his troubled past, but before he could start to recollect, the main story moved on to a radical Muslim cleric, sentenced to prison in Lebanon. Cam sat forward, all of his focus was now on the TV. He almost didn't notice the day-crew turn up.

'Morning everybody.' Diane said, in her usual cheery way. Following closely behind, Dave followed through the rest-room door.

'Hey Cam, how was your night?'

'Normal for me, couple of simple jobs, nothing too taxing.' He liked Dave; he had started a few months after Cam, so he was still relatively new and still a bit nervous about the job – probably the only thing they didn't have in common, as Cam never seemed to feel his nerves. Social situations and crowds made Cam uneasy, however, he had an ability to remain calm in almost all situations, and he had had his fair share of dangerous moments. He remembered back to Dave's first shift. He had had to respond to a lightning strike – Dave seemed to attract the tough jobs. When Cam turned up for work, everything calmed down. This was a running joke around the station. When he was on they could expect a quiet shift. Probably why people didn't mind working with him.

Pleasantries were exchanged and there was a quick handover of the ambulance, made easy as they hadn't used anything except some diesel, as they travelled between their 'non-jobs' as Cam called them. Soon it was time for home. The night-crew took their belongings out of the ambulance and grabbed their bags.

'Right then, have a good few days off and I'll see you next week,' Nick said. 'Anything planned?'

'Nah, just resting.' More lies. It was becoming a habit. Walking towards his car, Cam looked over at the hills in the distance. Picturesque, with the swaying trees in the foreground and the sound of babbling from the river behind them. 'Nice town,' he thought. Sometimes he found himself standing outside the station during night shifts, just taking it all in, enjoying the silence and listening to the river. He still felt lucky to be working in one of the most beautiful areas in the UK.

He drove home, through the national park. Snow had already begun to appear on the tops of the hills, just as it had when he arrived at the station for the first time. It had only been a year, yet somehow it felt like a long time ago.

Cam's home was a small annexe attached to Mr and Mrs Crossley's cottage, not at all big, but enough for him. Mrs Crossley was a pleasant-looking old lady who could always find something to talk about, but gave him the space he needed. His modest home was well kept and cosy, and with no electricity he always had a fire going. Mr and Mrs Crossley's old furniture filled the small living space. Well-worn wooden floors, warped and cracked from the heat of the fire, were marked by dripping candle wax. This simple life was one of the reasons why he had chosen this part of the country.

Cam pulled up outside the cottage. He felt mentally and physically exhausted. The newspapers of the day, lying on the passenger seat, had been bought at one of the newsagents that he passed on his way home. The newspapers had priority in his schedule – sleep came second on the task list.

'Morning Mrs Crossley,' Cam called, as she waved at him through the kitchen window. Finding the right key he opened his front door and quickly made his way in then slammed it shut behind him, so as not to let too much cold air inside. He threw the papers down on to the table and lit the fire; same old routine after every night shift. Cam was prepared, having cut the wood the day before; saving time was almost a hobby of Cam's. With the small room warming up, Cam poured himself a whisky. If anyone saw him they would think he was an alcoholic, but this was effectively his evening before bed.

'Right, let's get this done.' He started fanning through the papers until something leapt out at him. He nosed through the pages, finely tuned to what he was seeking. That morning he found it. 'Radical Muslim cleric sentenced to prison in Lebanon for raising funds for Al Qa'eda. He is in hiding in the UK to avoid his punishment.' Cam sipped his whisky as the flames flickered in the hearth. Whyte & Mackay – blended, but one of his favourites.

Carefully cutting round the article and setting it to one side, Cam thought to himself, 'Maybe they don't know where you are but I do!' Some of the other papers carried similar stories – and a very useful photo of the man. He kept this too.

Cam sat back in his chair and took another swig of his drink. He could feel the warmth of the whisky in his body now. He trusted the power of the amber liquid to help him sleep. Piled on the bookcase in the corner of the room were some board games: Cluedo, Monopoly, Risk and Trivial Pursuit. In the middle of the pile sat Scrabble. Not the best hiding place for his files, but sometimes the best hiding place was in plain sight.

Sliding back on his chair he made his way over to the bookshelf and pulled out the box. Inside there were a number of files, one with the name Abu-Al-Khayr Barakat written on it. Cam took out the cardboard folder and opened it, revealing a collage of newspaper cuttings. With the new articles and photos now glued alongside the others, Cam looked over the whole document. Plans made over the past few months were about to be carried out. Cam studied the face of the man on his latest photo.

'So, you're the first.'

Chapter 3

The train journey to Birmingham would take nearly four hours. Plenty of time to run through everything in his mind, just one more time. Attention to detail was paramount. Nothing could go wrong – so much of his life was at stake.

Covering his tracks had proved to be far harder than he had anticipated. Using public transport, paid for with cash, seemed to be the only way to get around undetected by electronic monitoring systems and CCTV cameras. With over four million CCTV cameras in the UK, the average person was caught on camera about three hundred times a day. You couldn't drive anywhere without your movements being monitored. He would stay out of high-crime areas and high-density population areas, where more surveillance devices were used by the authorities.

Cam had to be careful never to use his bank cards in places that could incriminate him. That was the simplest method of tracking anyone's movement around the country. He remembered his advanced vetting interview all those years ago, when he was asked about his most personal details. Had he ever used drugs? Did he have any strange sexual desires? Why had he withdrawn a large amount of money in a town far away from where he lived – and what had he spent it on? He had nothing to hide back then, but still the interviewer had found a way of making him feel guilty. Good at his job, he'd been.

For the past few months Cam had been asking for small amounts of cash back every time he went shopping. He had been putting it aside and would use it as payment for anything he might need while away.

After reviewing his notes, for what felt like the hundredth time, he finally slipped the document back into the folder and then his bag. He wondered if he was really going to do it. Once started down that dark road, turning back would not be an option. With the image of the man's face burned into his mind, Cam began to think about the first time he had taken a man's life. Still recovering from last night's shift, he closed his eyes, hoping to take a nap. Then he was back in the jungle.

* * * * * * *

That night it was so dark that it was impossible to see if there was anyone there. When the sun goes down in the jungle it is pitch black – nearly no ambient light, nothing for your eyes to adjust to. Ritchie had been a few metres to his right – far too close. The night made everyone move closer together. That was human instinct.

Cam knelt down to take a rest; he needed water. Reaching round, he pulled out one of his water bottles and took a few mouthfuls. The lukewarm water re-hydrated but didn't refresh. The heat in that place was unbearable. There was nowhere to go to get away from it, constantly wet from non-stop sweating; it was hard to take on more water than your body got rid of.

Cam could taste the salt on his lips and the sweat burned in his eyes.

'How can anyone fight in a place like this?' was all Cam could think. Between the heat, the darkness and above all the leeches, Sierra Leone was not a place he wanted to be. Totally exposed, he looked over at Ritchie, who motioned forward. They had no choice but to move on. It was going to be one of those nights. Parts of Freetown had once again been plunged into darkness as the so-called government cut the power to parts of the town. Some said it was to save electricity, but more probably it was to allow the rebels in.

Cam's small group of intelligence, linguists and communication specialists had been based in a small, fortified house called 'Seaview' on the outskirts of the city. Every once in a while the rebels would try to take back parts of the town – usually on nights like this one. Cam had spent many nights leaning out of one of the top-floor windows of 'Seaview', watching and listening, nervous on hearing the rebels moving around in the jungle that surrounded the house. As a five-man team they could easily have been overrun. Cam knew he would fight to the death. From what he had seen since he had arrived in the country, it would not be worth getting captured. These rebels were always high on drugs and could commit acts of extreme violence.

'One step at a time,' he thought, his four other senses sharpened due to the lack of vision. 'Slowly does it!' Cam felt sure he could hear his heart beating through his chest. They had to get to the infantry group stationed only a few miles from their house. When the power went down, so had their lines of communication to the Gurkhas – the team's only form of help. He and Ritchie had to get to them and arrange some transportation for the rest of the team. Important equipment and documents could not be left behind for the enemy.

Unsure whether his eyes were playing tricks on him, he moved silently towards the dark shapes in the distance. 'Is that someone there? I see some movement.'

It was after the city's curfew – perhaps it was the Sierra Leone National Army at one of their check-points. Then it happened.

There's no sound like that of an AK47 being fired in your direction. It has an unmistakeable, loud, metallic crack. Both Ritchie and Cam instinctively dived to the ground; both crawled into cover behind trees, and lay as flat and as still as they could. If it had been possible, Cam would have dug a hole in which to hide. The whiz and crack of the rounds flying over their heads was enough evidence that this was very accurate fire.

'British Army, don't shoot!' Ritchie was shouting at the top of his voice, in the hope that it was the SLNA. The silence that followed lasted less than a second before the firing re-started.

Cam had the awful realisation that these were rebels, and they wanted to kill them. Soon the tree which Cam was cowering behind was being hit. Splinters of wood and bark showered down on him. Then, just as suddenly as it started, the firing stopped. Cam peered round his shattered tree. Surprisingly he could see better – perhaps the adrenaline improved his night vision. There were two of them – he could see their silhouettes. Both were struggling to change their magazines. Ritchie caught Cam's gaze, and instantly they knew what had to be done.

Now in a kneeling position, leaning on the splintered tree, he raised his weapon into his shoulder. Taking aim down his sights, he felt anger towards these two amateurs. 'How dare they take us on! How dare they think they could kill us! We are better than they could ever be!'

Cam was an excellent shot – he always had been. With the shadowy figures in his iron sight, he squeezed the trigger. Single rapid fire, round after round. Although he could not see Ritchie,

Cam knew he was doing the same. He had no idea how many shots he had fired before he finally stopped. Lowering his rifle he waited for movement. Nothing. He had definitely seen them go down. Looking at each other Cam and Ritchie knew now was not the time to hang around; they had to get out of there. In an instant they were up and running, changing magazines as they were moving. Cam was surprised how his training automatically took over. Once he had a fresh magazine in his rifle, he slid the empty one down his half-opened shirt. At a safe distance they stopped.

'You OK?'

'Yeah, you?'

'Yeah, do you think we got them?' Cam asked.

'Well, I didn't see them get back up.'

Cam knew he hadn't missed – he never did.

'OK, let's get going, we're nearly there,' said Ritchie. 'Keep your eyes open and better spacing. Move.' As they moved off he thought, 'It was either them or me. And it wasn't going to be me.'

* * * * * * *

The Adl Ghaffari Mosque was in the suburbs of Birmingham, in an area called Small Heath – a mostly Muslim part of the town and a pleasant area to live in with very little crime. The locals were friendly, even to the obvious outsider sitting in the park across the street from the mosque. The Adl Ghaffari Islamic Centre had funded and built this park for the community. It was good to see. Such a shame a few bad apples could give that peaceful religion a bad name.

Hours had passed and he knew he had been sitting there far too long. It was going to start looking suspicious. Looking around for a new place where he could watch unseen, he spotted a building, a schoolhouse converted into desirable flats. The building had an old flight of metal stairs leading to the roof. After crossing the street and ascending the staircase, he looked across the rooftop. The building was deserted and had a low wall, perfect for watching over. He found a few bricks to sit on, giving him just enough extra height to see over the wall. Now it was a waiting game.

He knew who he was looking for – a man called Affan Jabour. He was a member of the mosque's council and therefore spent most of his days there. This man was innocent, guilty of nothing more than being a relative of Abu-Al-Khayr Barakat – the man everyone was looking for. Barakat was an Al Qa'eda fundraiser. He was also a known terrorist, and had been involved in many atrocious acts of death and destruction. Barakat had blood on his hands.

Cam had information that linked these two men. Before leaving the military, Cam had taken copies of classified documents with information about all terror suspects in the UK. This was a serious crime and could land him in jail if it was ever found out. These documents revealed their suspected crimes, what they were known to have done and every movement they had made while in the UK.

As the light began to fade, the temperature dropped. Cam pulled his coat up around his neck. Every time the door to the mosque opened, Cam looked up, hoping to see the relative. Nothing. Soon it would be too dark to see from that distance and he would have to find another vantage point.

Cam stood up, about to leave his position when two men walked through the door on to the street. He stopped and watched. They stood for a short time, having a conversation. Cam stood on the rooftop, straining through the low light to see who it was. 'That looks like him,' he thought. A little older than the photos he had, but most definitely him. He rushed down the metal stairs as fast as he could to street level. From the shadows of the alley, he could see the two men talking to each other across the park.

The two men finally said their farewells and walked off in different directions. At a safe distance Cam broke cover and followed. Jabour was heading off in an easterly direction. He was wearing smart trousers, expensive shoes and a long black coat, making him easy to follow at an extended distance. In one hand he carried a paper bag.

The man was heading home. Cam already knew where he lived. His aim was to gather as much information about him as possible. Keeping a good distance, Cam began to get a familiar feeling – all the surveillance exercises he had done those many years ago, following practice suicide bombers down Edinburgh's main street. He had all the covert experience in the world. He knew how to blend in, what type of clothes to wear – no logos, since people automatically read what's on t-shirts. No bright colours; no light-coloured shoes, as all people will see is a white pair of shoes walking down the street. He knew all the tricks.

Also, he had to be aware of anti-surveillance techniques. Sometimes terrorist groups used dickers. These guys would surround the target and watch for people trailing, but this was highly unlikely here tonight.

The feeling of being let down by the government was as strong as ever. Cam had been a member of a highly elite team of surveillance experts, trained for dangerous anti-terrorist operations; the group was called Charlie Troop. Cam's particular speciality had been covert infiltration. The team had been involved in tackling the potential suicide-bomber threat in the UK, and for this they had been well trained in the most up-to-date bomb-disposal techniques. During a training exercise for a suicide-bomb scenario, a horrible truth came out.

The boss of the troop gathered the men and began to explain that, in the event of a real attack, the possibility was that COBRA, the collection of government officials, were unlikely to order the killing of a suicide-bomber on the streets of the UK. This would be seen as murder as the bomber would be innocent right up until the point he set the device off – meaning they would probably let the first one go! Then the government would have the backing of the public to do what had to be done the next time it happened. No thought about the destruction of one of the UK's major city centres, or the death and horrific injuries it would cause. The fatalities in Cam's team would be high. The scene played back in Cam's head as if it had been the previous day.

'If anybody wants out,' the boss said, 'now is the time. No one will think any less of you.' Nobody wanted out – this was what they were there for, and their silence was all the confirmation the boss needed. 'One more thing,' the boss continued, 'the police won't allow us to carry our weapons. They are too worried about us tapping the bastards – so potentially you will be unarmed.'

They were right to worry; no one in the team would think twice about taking the target out, if it meant it would save lives, especially their own. Better to be tried by twelve, than carried by six.

'However, keep this between us – I will make sure you're armed,' said the boss. 'Just remember, it will be seen as murder and you most likely face prison.'

* * * * * * *

That was the moment Cam realised the UK government was weak. Not one of them was prepared to risk loosing their jobs, even if it meant death and destruction for the general public. If the job of protecting the innocent was to be done properly, he would have to take matters into his own hands.

Chapter 4

'Focus. Must focus. Now is not the time to let your mind wander. This is the time for concentration.' With the target making his way towards his home, Cam followed like a ghost. 'So far so good,' Cam thought, as he looked around. He scanned the corners of buildings and randomly placed lamp posts for cameras. He did not need to be caught on CCTV following the relative of the man who was about to be all over the news. Luckily the area around the mosque and Affan Jabour's house was a safe place to live, and had very little need to be covered by police.

At that time of the day it was easy to stay inconspicuous. The crowds of people on the streets, as they left their places of work, steadily grew, providing many hiding places. However, that can also help the target. If they want to disappear, that time of day is perfect, but Jabour displayed no sign that he thought he might be being followed. He was taking the most direct route home. He wasn't crossing the road, changing direction or suddenly stopping, such as to look into shop windows. He was simply walking home.

Weaving between the pedestrians, Cam tried to keep up with his target. Then he was gone! He only lost sight of him for a second – then he vanished. 'Where the hell did he go?' thought Cam. 'He must have entered one of the shops on the street.' Cam increased his speed, desperate to know where he went. As he drew closer he could see that Jabour had stopped at a clothing shop, a well-known one. 'Damn it!' Cam couldn't go in after him; those places were always completely covered by cameras to catch shoplifters. He walked straight past.

In the few seconds that it took to walk by the shop, Cam took in as much information as possible. He strained to see the entire shop out of the corner of his eye, not wanting to turn his head and be seen looking in. He saw Jabour at the returns counter, handing over a pair of jeans. There were cameras everywhere; every inch of the shop floor was covered. Now past the store, Cam crossed the road. He needed a good view of the main entrance. Once again he was in the shadow of an alley; he could see the door to the clothes shop, now all he could do was wait. Cam hoped he would walk out the door.

Soon enough he left the shop. Away from the centre of the suburb the streets were less busy. The stalk resumed. Cam knew that the longer the chase went on, the greater the risk of him looking suspicious. Not far from his home, Jabour made another stop – the Jalfrazi House. 'Must be stopping for his dinner,' Cam thought. Still on the opposite side of the street from his target he crossed the road, heading directly towards the takeaway. Jabour spoke into his phone. What wouldn't he have paid to be in on that conversation?! Checking the layout of the curry house, Cam spotted only one camera, covering the counter, not the door. He entered the takeaway and headed for the corner of the waiting area. Grabbing a menu he sat down to read it. Cam knew he had taken a risk, but he was not on camera, and Jabour had not noticed him enter.

Cam listened to him place an order; it was for someone else. He then put his mobile phone into his pocket and placed an order for himself. Jabour took a seat two to the left of Cam. Far too close for comfort. Cam could do nothing but sit and wait – but this looked suspicious. To Cam's relief, Jabour showed no interest in him. Cam looked at his watch and made a noise suggesting impatience, hoping to give the impression that he was waiting for someone or something. It seemed the only thing he could do.

Jabour got up to take his order from the woman behind the counter, so close Cam could smell his aftershave. Jabour said goodbye. Noting that the man seemed very polite, Cam followed again. 'I must keep a longer distance between us now.' Entering his house and closing the door behind him signalled the end of the stalk. Cam backed off to the far end of the street; he would go nowhere near his house tonight. 'Who was he talking to on his phone? Why a take away for two?' Affan was known to live alone.

There would be no more work that night, but Cam had plenty to think about. Only one more stop before heading back to his accommodation for a well earned rest. It was 6pm, and closing time for the clothes shop. Cam waited for the last member of staff to leave and lock up. The lights went out. He hoped that meant that the cameras were off, or at the very least, that the store interior would be too dark for details to show up. The manager's assistant was closing the metal shutters as Cam approached.

'Excuse me, I know it's late and you're closing up, but I think I lost my wallet in the changing rooms earlier today.'

'Oh, I'm sorry but I'm about to lock up and can't go back in or the alarm will be set off,' she said, tilting her head to one side.

'Please, I really need my wallet – I can't leave it overnight. Is there no way you can quickly have a look to see if it's there? I'm hoping it's been handed in.' He replied, slightly mimicking the woman's stance and putting on a mild Birmingham accent. Cam had a way of getting people to do as he needed. Affability got him a long way.

'Well, OK. Just wait here and I'll be back in a few minutes.'

'Thank you very much,' Cam said, as she ducked under the half-closed shutters.

He waited a few seconds then followed, making his way to the returns counter with his head down in case the cameras were still recording. The lights were off on the shop floor. Cam breathed easily, confident that he was almost invisible. Over the other side of the counter was a rail with returned items hanging on metal coat hangers. Only one pair of jeans was on the rail. Cam checked the pockets. Nothing. Looking at the size, he noted they were a 42 waist. He put the jeans back and silently slipped out under the shutters.

'Sorry, no wallet in the lost-and-found box.' She seemed genuinely sorry for the man who was still standing outside.

'OK, never mind. I'll find it. Must be somewhere I've been today. Thanks for looking. Bye.'

As he turned and walked away he considered what he had discovered so far. Two takeaways when Jabour lived alone, and a pair of jeans that were far too big for him, returned to a shop. Jabour couldn't be more than a size 34, and he was on the short side. No way would he accidentally buy himself a pair of jeans that big. 'I know who is around a size 42: Barakat.'

Chapter 5

He had to find a way in. The average terraced house had to have a weak spot. Although there had been no signs of movement since Jabour left for work that morning, Cam was certain that Barakat was in there. But if he suspected that, who else did? Were the intelligence services there? Were they watching too?

Having completed a sweep of the area around the residence of his target, he concluded they were not. No vehicles coming and going or stopping in the street. Nobody hanging around. The rooftops were clear and the windows overlooking the property didn't have anything out of the ordinary going on behind them… but he could never be sure. If anything should alert him that any agency was watching, it would have to be called off.

Sipping on his takeaway coffee, he made another pass by the house. The front door had a large porch, making the entrance to the property rather dark. However, probably to combat this, the owner had installed a movement sensor and this would activate the intruder-light, illuminating the main entrance. The door itself looked simple enough: one lock, a standard pin and tumbler system, a doorbell and a thick 'welcome' mat.

Modern windows had been recently installed on both floors. Both doors and windows seemed to be connected to an alarm system. The flashing box high up on the side of the building could be a fake, but Cam could not take that chance. Most alarms were connected to monitoring services. Jabour's system was handled by Household Security; a company like that would alert the police to a possible break-in. Also, some firms would send their own security guards round to secure the property. Alarms could be set to 'silent', so the intruder would be unaware that an alarm had been set off, allowing them to be caught red-handed.

Gathering information like this always took all day. At least a few hours had to be put between runs past the target, otherwise someone might start to notice. Soon the light would start to fade and Cam wanted to get one more full view of the house before leaving. Standing on the other side of the street was the only place to see the whole building. He didn't like it and felt exposed, so he would only linger for a second or two while trying to take in as much as he could.

The white building was a corner house on a quiet suburban street. The roof space had been converted into another floor. A closed curtain blocked any view into the loft conversion. Around the corner was a wall about seven feet high that separated the property's courtyard from the street. The phone lines entered the house at this point through a junction box.

His time was up; he had to go. Walking away Cam knew exactly how he was going to get in. He had done things like this before – but not illegally as this was going to be. The last time it was his job.

* * * * * * *

He had to hurry. It was approaching the same time that Jabour left the mosque the day before. With the light fading around him, Cam felt more at ease – he was always more comfortable in the dark, where he couldn't be seen. For the plan to work he would need Jabour's mobile telephone number.

Rushing through the alleys to avoid as many cameras as he could, he arrived on the same street as the mosque – but he had to be careful as he didn't want to run face to face with his target. The alley in which he began his stalk last night would do – he could watch and wait from there.

Jabour was a little later than the previous night, but Cam could wait. On the way there he spotted a phone box on the corner of the street. As soon as Jabour left the mosque he would head towards it. It would be much easier if Cam could have used his own mobile, but most modern mobiles had GPS trackers in them – and he didn't want anyone tracking him.

Jabour finally left the mosque and headed off in the same direction as the previous night, back towards his house. He was setting patterns – another sign he didn't consider that he was being watched. Cam emerged from the shadows and made his way to the phone box.

'118 118, how can I help you?'

'Can you connect me to the Adl Ghaffari Mosque in Small Heath, Birmingham please?'

'Yes, Sir, connecting you now.'

'Thank you.' Cam listened to the ring-tone and looked down the street towards the mosque's main entrance. 'I'm about to enter the mosque,' he thought.

'Centre for Islamic Studies,' said the voice in the public phone's earpiece.

'Hello, my name is Dr Sam Cooper. I'm a consultant at Birmingham's Queen Elizabeth hospital. I need to speak to

Mr Affan Jabour.' He felt as if he was virtually inside the mosque.

That was further than he ever got when he was in the military. Many requests by his team to be allowed to conduct covert reconnaissance inside mosques were all refused. The government's response was that the ground inside a mosque was the property of the people of Islam, so any non-believer found inside would cause an international incident. Frustration at not being able to get in burned him up. Cam knew he could get in, reveal what was going on inside and get out, leaving no trace of his movements.

That was what he was for – he had an ability to blend in, disappear. He was silent and cunning and his insertion skills were second to none.

'I'm sorry, Mr Jabour has just left. Can I take a message?'

'I really need to speak to him, it's quite urgent. Is there any way of contacting him?' Cam felt sure it was a peaceful place. 'No terrorist cells in there. Always follow your gut instinct.' Cam lived by this, and it had saved his life more than once.

There was one mosque Cam remembered that was a confirmed weapon store and possible bomb factory. Rumours were circulating that young Muslims were being groomed to be suicide bombers. And still they were refused permission to recce it. Now he was on his own, he could do things his way – he could do what desperately needed to be done.

'I have a landline and a mobile number for Mr Jabour, however, he has instructed me not to pass out his mobile number. Would his home number be any help?'

'Sorry, I have his home number on his notes. And there's no answer. I really need to speak to him now.' After a short pause the operator continued.

'Can I ask what it is about?'

'I'm sorry that, due to patient-doctor confidentiality, I can't discuss this with anyone but him.'

'OK, I have this mobile number for him: 07523 361315.'

'Thank you very much. I'm sure Mr Jabour will appreciate your help.'

'Thank you Sir, goodbye.' As soon as the phone was hung up, a thought occurred to him. The operator would probably speak to Jabour the next day, since Cam had made it sound very important. And if no doctor had called he would know something was out of the ordinary. Standing in the phone box, he tried desperately to adapt his plan.

There was no way out of it. He had to act that night.

* * * * * * *

Planning and preparation – very important. Cam had to think about every action he was going to take that night. Everything had to be covered; the last thing he wanted was to need something and to have left it behind. Cam was an over-planner; he tended to carry too much, far more than he needed. But not that night; he had to be light; too many trappings meant too much noise, and the aim was to remain silent. He stood in his small, drab hotel room and ran over the list in his head.

Piece by piece, Cam slipped his equipment into his bag. Small screwdriver set and his leatherman – he would need both of those. Home-made lock-pick set for gaining entry. Not as good as a factory-made set of professional lock-picks, but he didn't want to be registered as owning a set of picks. Spare gloves – he would be using his black leather aircrew gloves.

Also some latex gloves for when greater dexterity was necessary. A small blanket about one metre square and some shoe covers, like the ones workmen wear over their boots. Also a camera flash screen and his NVGs. Cam used Cobra Tornado Night Vision goggles; they were expensive but top of the range and small.

He laid out his dark trousers and black hooded top on the back of a chair. Into the pocket of his top he slid a black balaclava and his first pair of leather gloves. Only one more item was needed. Reaching up, he felt around on the top of the wardrobe. Gripping the cold metal object he lifted it down – an old Browning HP pistol with a sound-suppressor attached. A weapon with which he was very familiar. It was also untraceable; he had brought it home after finding it in Sierra Leone. It was rusty and didn't work at first, but with a bit of care and attention he had restored it. Getting hold of a sound-suppressor had been more challenging. Although they could be purchased over the internet, he didn't want any trace of him buying weapon parts. It was a long process, and he had to convince the owner of the weapon shop that it was for a display model. Cam had bought a decommissioned Browning and had produced it to prove that the suppressor would be on a weapon that had its firing-pin cut, rendering it inoperable.

There was nothing more to do now but wait, try to get some sleep and mentally prepare for the night's activities. He lay down to rest; he would aim to be at Jabour's house at about 2 am. At that time of night the human body was naturally most at rest. The average person slept in blocks of four hours, then woke up for perhaps just seconds and would go straight back to sleep. Therefore Cam would try to complete the first half of his plan for about 3 am, then wait for the occupants of the house to go back to sleep before finishing the job.

Cam hoped that he would be able to slip out of his B&B without being noticed to make the trip to Small Heath. As before, he would use a taxi to get him in the vicinity of the target, and make the rest of the journey on foot. He lay down on the bed with a squeak of the springs and reached over for his alarm clock. He had owned that old cheap alarm clock for years, it had been everywhere with him. With the alarm set he drifted off into a sound sleep.

* * * * * * *

The journey was brief, taking less time than on other occasions. At one o'clock in the morning there was little or no traffic. Cam felt warmed by the orange glow of the passing street lights. Although the darkness was Cam's best tool, he was comforted by artificial light.

He had chosen the route with great care. The taxi would only go as far as CCTV coverage. Once there were no more between Cam and the target he would get out. The taxi would hide him from the authorities. He paid the driver and the car accelerated away. As the taxi drove off Cam felt the familiar sensation of being alone. Most people would feel uncomfortable, but for Cam this was where he belonged. When he was alone he knew nothing would go wrong – other people made mistakes, not him.

A ten-minute walk and Cam was at the house. The street was deserted and Cam knew it was time. Within moments he was in the side-street and leaning on the wall next to the house. In the shadows between the street lights he looked up to the telephone junction box. This small grey box on the outside wall was the network interface for the telephone connection. As he looked up he thought, 'If I climb this wall, it's started and there will be no turning back.' Cam realised his life was about to change. At that point he could still return to his comfortable easy life – he could walk away, or he could make the difference he was never allowed to in the military.

Decision made, he had the chance to save lives. One last look down the street – nothing. Turning to face the wall he jumped up and gripped the top, then in one smooth motion he pulled himself up. Keeping as low as he could, he shuffled along the top of the wall towards the side of the house. Next to the network interface box. He reached into his pocket and put on a pair of latex gloves. Leave no trace. Out of the bag came his leatherman tool. He clipped the twisted metal tie and levered open the plastic lid. He kept close to the side of the house to mask his movements. He knew that inside every network interface box was a short cable terminating in a jack plug, which connected the house to the phone system. The plug was a similar design to interior phone plugs, all Cam had to do was depress the clip and pull it from its housing. Once done, the power to the house's phone lines was cut.

'OK, let's test how sensitive the alarm is.' Cam closed the hatch to the network box. Raising his arm he pushed against the frame of the window. Nothing, pushing a little bit harder, still nothing. 'Can't make too much noise, there must be another way to set it off.' Down in the courtyard Cam could see the back door of the house. It was old and wooden – possibly alarmed. It was very dark down there and Cam had been on the wall far too long. Silently he jumped down, taking the impact of the landing in his thighs. He felt safer in the darkness of the courtyard – he could take his time now. In case he needed a fast way out of the yard, he unlocked the gate at the rear, allowing him access to the back road. Cam slipped on his leather gloves, reached down and gripped the door handle. Slowly he turned the faded brass handle down, inch by inch until it stopped. It didn't yield. The door was old, and had been affected by the damp, so was not an exact fit to the frame. Pushing it inwards there was just enough movement to slightly separate the magnetic connectors that initiated the alarm. The quiet of the night was interrupted by the shrill scream of the alarm. Cam quickly but calmly turned and walked out of the yard, and took a left towards a phone box a few yards down the street.

After a few minutes the alarm was silenced. Cam now had to become an operator from Household Security, the security company that should now know about a possible break-in at the house in Small Heath. With the power to the phone line cut they would be none the wiser.

'Hello, am I speaking to Mr Jabour?'

'Yes, who am I speaking to?'

'My name is Sam, I am calling from Household Security, we have an alarm at your property and we are calling to find out if everything is OK, and to let you know police are on the way to have a look around your property.'

'Why, that's not necessary, I'm sure there is nothing to worry about, it just went off by accident.'

'OK Mr Jabour. If you would like I can stand down the police and instead I will send over our own security specialists in the morning. They will look into the reason why the alarm has been set off.'

'OK, OK goodbye.'

'One last thing Mr Jabour. The reason I'm calling you on your mobile is your land-line has been blocked. Your alarm system automatically contacts us. Can I have your four digit pass code so I can free up your line?'

'I don't think I've given you one, I don't remember ever being asked to.'

'If one has not been set up, it will be the same as the code you enter into your system to cancel your alarm.'

'Right, right, 4929.'

'Thank you Mr Jabour, your line is now reset and you should expect our security staff in the morning. Thank you and good night.'

'Good night.'

Cam had a strong feeling Jabour would not want police to be looking around his house, if he was hiding a wanted man.

This was the point that Cam did not like – he had to reconnect the phone line as soon as he could. If Jabour tested his line he would discover that it had been cut off.

Back to the wall he glanced over the windows overlooking the rear courtyard. Everything seemed quiet, no movement. Within seconds he was up on the wall and shutting the network box after reconnecting the power. Cam froze when he heard the handle of the back door rattle. Someone on the inside was moving the handle. If the door were to open, Cam could be spotted. He was only a couple of feet above the door. But the door did not move. 'Just testing it, maybe their alarm can locate the door or window that was disturbed.' Cam waited silently, still crouched on the wall. 'That means they have not reset the alarm and possibly not tested the phone line.' Cam was convinced he had got away with it. He had succeeded in cutting their line, got their alarm code and reconnected the phone line. And as far as the occupants of the house were concerned, nothing was wrong. Jumping down from the wall he disappeared into the dark of the night to wait for everything to settle down before continuing with his plan.

Chapter 6

It was another clear winter night, without a cloud in the sky to hold in the warmth. The temperature had dropped dramatically. The clothing he was dressed in was chosen for a purpose, thin and close-fitting, allowing him to move quietly without making unnecessary noise. It was not designed to keep out the cold.

Trying not to shiver in the darkness, Cam concentrated on the house. The lights had been out now for over half an hour, and there had been no movement in the windows. He was interested in the room in the converted attic, since he had seen the outline of someone looking out into the street, when the lights went out on the ground floor. There had to be at least two people in the house and Cam was sure that one of them was the man he was looking for.

It was time; the house was sleeping. With his lock-pick set in one hand and the camera flash screen folded up in his other, he broke cover out of the shadows and into the orange glow of the street lights. Moving closer towards the house, he slipped the lock-pick set into the pocket of his hooded top and pulled the hood up over his head.

The front door was shrouded in darkness, giving him plenty of cover. All he had to do was overcome the first hurdle – the sensor. If he got that wrong the intruder-light would illuminate him like a rabbit caught in headlights. Turning off the street and facing the house, Cam crouched down making himself as small as possible.

With the grip on the camera flash screen released, it flipped open into a round silver reflective shield. Hiding behind the screen he inched forward towards the sensor. Concentrating on keeping his entire body behind the screen he dissolved into the shadows of the doorway. The passive infrared sensor would measure infrared light radiating from objects in its field of view. The camera flash screen would reflect these and protect Cam from being detected as he moved. The closer he got, the higher he lifted his shield until it was right in front of the sensor. He jammed the edges of the screen into the gaps between bricks either side of the sensor and slowly letting go to make sure the screen was secure, he knew he was safe in the blackness of the doorway. Turning towards the door he had plenty of time – picking locks could be time-consuming.

Automatically he straddled the welcome mat, placing his feet on either side. Always suspicious of booby traps – he hated that term – he knew pressure mats could be used to alert occupants that there was a stranger on their property. Squatting down to get a good view of the lock, he took out his pick set.

As he opened the leather pouch, he remembered making his pick set from the discarded metal strips found at the side of the road. The thin metal strips that had broken off street-sweeper brushes were perfect for creating picks. He had carefully shaped the ends of the strips into the various picks and tension rods, and had practised on any lock he could find to hone the skills he had first learned years ago in the military.

Cam inserted the tension rod into the keyhole, turning the plug in the same direction, as if he had the key. He had created a sideways tension on the pins in the lock shaft. Next he chose the appropriate pick and slid it into the keyhole. Feeling for the first pin, he used the shaped end of the pick to lift the pin. A slight click confirmed that he had found the right level for the pin, as if the correct key had been inserted. Moving on to the next pin, he repeated the process and continued until all the pins were in position on the small ledge created inside the lock by the turning of the tension rod. When the last one was in place the lock turned.

With the door unlocked he returned the pick set to his bag, and out came the small blanket and some shoe covers. With his bag on his back he considered the door. It was modern and should open smoothly and silently. The door opened and immediately he spotted the flashing box on the wall. '4929. I hope it's still the correct code.' With the code entered using the rubber keypad, the flashing stopped.

The warmth in the passageway spilled out past Cam and into the night. After taking a good look into the hallway, he spread out the small blanket on the floor just inside the doorway. Standing on the edge of the blanket, he closed the door behind him. 'I'm in!' He stood as still as possible, breathing quietly and listening for sounds of movement. The house was silent.

Cam pulled the shoe covers out of his pocket and put them on over his boots; he would leave no trace that he had been here. The covers were a tight fit so they wouldn't make any sound as he moved. 'Can't see much... my night vision still hasn't adjusted to the low light.' He needed to find a safe place to hide until he could see more. The small passageway led straight to the living room.

He picked up the blanket and moved silently forward. Pausing in the entrance to the room he noted a large chair in the corner. Manoeuvring in behind the chair he placed the blanket on the floor and sat down cross-legged. Here he would wait until his eyes adjusted to the dark.

* * * * * * *

Cam's eyes gradually adjusted to the dark, and he was able to have a good look around the room he had been sitting in. He had been there for about twenty minutes. Eyes normally took about twenty or thirty minutes to fully adjust to dark conditions.

A well-looked-after living room – religious decorations covered the walls and shelves. From his hiding place behind the corner chair he could see a large couch, an oblong coffee table and some shelving displaying miscellaneous items. He had plenty of room to move around without disturbing anything. The floor was carpeted; he could tread silently. To avoid making unwanted noise he would stay close to the walls, minimising the risk of any squeaking or cracking.

Once his eyes had fully adjusted to the darkness, it was time to make his way upstairs. Cam stood up and picked up his blanket, folding it and sliding it under the shoulder strap of his bag. Keeping as close as he could to the wall he made his way towards the door at the far side of the room, which opened into another corridor leading to the stairs. Looking the other way along the corridor, he could see the older back door that would lead to the courtyard at the rear of the house. This was the alarmed old wooden door that he had utilised on his previous visit. Opposite the living room was another door that had to lead to the kitchen. No need to go in there. The occupants were fast asleep and the bedrooms were upstairs.

One step at a time, placing his feet at either edge of the steps so that they wouldn't creak if loose, he made his way to the first floor. When his head reached floor height he could see the layout of the landing. Three closed doors led off it. Cam would have to have a look behind all of them.

Only two were bedrooms. One had the light switch outside the door on the landing, indicating that it was the bathroom. He was close to at least one of the occupants of the house and it was crucial to move as silently as possible. He had to concentrate on every step towards the first door. Bending his knees slightly to provide more suspension to his steps, he allowed each foot to make contact with the floor. Heel first, rolling slowly towards his toes on the outer edge of his foot. He remembered the technique of tightening muscles in the pelvis to give stronger control while moving slowly. At each step he moved his legs round in a slight semi circle to avoid his feet or knees rubbing against each other. He could feel the anticipation and nervous energy buzzing louder and louder as he approached the bedroom door.

Taking a firm stance, Cam placed his gloved hands on either side of the frame, then leaned in to listen against the door. With his ear less than an inch away he could hear muffled snoring on the other side. To stop any possible squeaking, Cam applied upwards pressure on the handle as he turned it. Alleviating any downward force on the hinges would stop the two parts grinding against each other. Clasping the handle and turning it all the way, so the bolt was completely withdrawn from its housing, he opened the door millimetres at a time. With the door opened a centimetre or so, he checked around the doorframe. There was nothing behind the door that could alert the occupant to his presence. No change to the snoring, except that it was slightly louder now the door was open.

From the open doorway Cam could now see the bed from which the snoring came. He could tell right away that the man in the bed was Affan Jabour, the owner of the house. No need to go any further there. With the door now closed, Cam pulled it firmly against the frame, so that when the bolt was released it wouldn't snap back into place. Older doors could do that when they didn't fit well.

He released the handle quietly and moved on, repeating the slow, silent progress along the landing.

Missing what was evidently the bathroom door he reached the last door. Pressing his ear to it he could hear nothing. Glancing around, he could not see any sign of more stairs, but there was definitely another floor. His man had to be up there. The room proved to be some sort of office. On the far side of the room, a set of stairs with no banister led up to another door. He wanted to leave a clear route of escape so he placed his rolled-up blanket at the bottom of the doorframe, so it would prevent the door from slamming shut – sometimes pressure built up in houses and it could slam doors shut as others opened, and Cam could not afford for that to happen.

Sneaking around the edge of the room, he listened to every sound. The house was still quiet as the sound of Affan snoring had now faded away. He moved cautiously up the stairs to the door at the top. Listening he could hear nothing. He lowered his hand to the bottom of the door; he could feel warm air, not cold, on his bare wrist. The room was lived in, and not used as an attic or storage space.

With the handle turned down all the way he began to push the wooden door open. Cam froze as he heard the creak of the door hinges. Standing as still as possible, he strained his ears – hoping to hear nothing. Relief. No movement, nothing. Cam placed his other hand in the centre of the door and pressing forward firmly, he hinged it open. The extra pressure worked – the door stopped creaking.

The man lying in the bed was sound asleep, unaware that an intruder was in his room. This man was much bigger than Jabour – this was what he expected. But Cam needed a closer look to confirm his identity. He couldn't afford a mistake, so at the risk of discovery, he crept towards the head of the bed. Crouching low, foot over foot with his arms out for balance, he sneaked sideways towards the face in the bed. The closer he got, the greater the risk that the man might wake – he might be a light sleeper. Cam visualised the location of his gun. On the left side of his bag was a net with an elastic band for carrying water-bottles, also handy for holding silenced pistols. If he should wake, Cam could draw the gun in one smooth movement over his shoulder.

Right up close to the man's face, he stopped to squat down, elbows on his knees. He hunched over. Barakat! His distinctive beard gave him away. He'd seen enough photos of the man to be sure that it was him. He hated him and everything he stood for. He took a few slow steps backwards, then made his way past the bottom of the bed to the other side. Still looking at the back of the sleeping man's head, he drew the pistol from its makeshift holster, straightened up and took aim.

However he tried to justify it, the act was cold-blooded murder. But this man was the murderer. He was a known terrorist, suspected of having involvement with the Bali bombings back in 2002. He was an active Al Qa'eda fundraiser – and that's why the authorities wanted him. He might also have been planning something in the UK. If he were to be caught, he might go to prison, but these guys had a way of postponing the inevitable, claiming the western world was against them for reasons of religious persecution. To take this monster out of the equation he had to take matters into his own hands. He was reminded of an observation by the philosopher Edmund Burke – that all that was necessary for evil to succeed was for good men to do nothing.

Thump, thump. The double tap was the most effective way of ensuring the target was dead. Cam holstered the smoking pistol, then took a moment to think about what he had done. Looking at the man's broken head he could see blood soaking into the pillowcase and sheets. He had rid the world of a dangerous man. Bending down, he picked up the two spent cartridges and put one into each trouser pocket so they wouldn't clink together as he moved. He couldn't leave them behind – they could be used to identify the gun that fired the shots. He did not want to jeopardise any of his future activities.

Without looking back he left the room, completely focused now on getting out undetected. Halfway down the stairs into the office room one of the stairs creaked. Subconsciously the adrenaline was making him speed up. 'Must slow down. Concentrate.' Passing his blanket door-stop he stooped and picked it up, replacing it between the bag straps and his body. Soon he was back in the hall by the alarm control box. As he entered 4929 into the key-pad, the box flashed once again. Cam knew he had fifteen or so seconds to exit the house. In one swift movement he opened the front door, spun round into the fresh outside air and quickly closed it. With his crime sealed inside the house he grabbed the camera shield that had been covering the movement sensor. He took a few steps away from the front door and was lit up as if the sun had risen early. His night vision was now ruined, but it didn't matter – he was leaving.

Seconds later he was on the street, walking away. It was early morning and in a few hours it would be sunrise. Wondering what the day would bring, Cam removed his shoe-covers and stuffed them into his trouser pocket. He thought about how to get back to the bed and breakfast. Strangely enough, this was one thing he forgot to consider, but how hard could it be to find another taxi?

* * * * * *

The sun was just rising as Cam let himself back into the bed and breakfast. Nobody was up yet, so he simply went back to his room, where he would wait until it was time to go down for breakfast.

Cam turned on the shower heater and while the water was warming up he packed his backpack. He placed everything he had used the previous night, including the clothes he wore, into the bag. He'd already packed the rest of his belongings into his holdall, except for a set of clothes, now folded on the foot of the bed, that he would wear for the journey home. Cam was ready to leave.

The warm water poured over his head and collected in the bottom of the shower. He had put the plug in so it would gradually fill up and warm his feet. With the adrenaline wearing off Cam could feel the familiar feeling of fatigue. He looked forward to having something to eat, and then the train journey back up north.

He stepped out of the shower dried himself and dressed. When it was time he made his way down into the dining room. The other guests had not emerged from their rooms for breakfast yet. Cam had placed an advance order for a 'full English' and was sitting watching the news in the dining area. So far there had been no mention of anything happening in Birmingham. However, it was only ten to eight and the crime might not have been discovered yet. He thought that it might be one of the first reports at the turn of the hour.

Sitting alone in the dining room his eyes felt heavy, as if they had sand in them. He was so tired. The warm feeling of exhaustion wrapped around him like a duvet and only the sound of the morning news being recapped roused him from his lethargy.

As he ate his breakfast, he focused his full concentration on the television in the corner of the room. Surely a murder would make the news – but still nothing was mentioned. He finished his breakfast and sat waiting for the story to break. 'It's possible that the body hasn't been discovered yet,' he thought. Perhaps Jabour didn't normally see Barakat before he left for work. He would have no reason to believe that anyone had been in his house during the night. Cam would have to wait until he was back home before he could check the news again.

After paying for his accommodation he took a taxi to the train station. Everything paid for by cash – no electronic trail. With his holdall high up on his shoulder he walked through the station. The holdall would hide his face from the CCTV cameras that he had spotted as he arrived in Birmingham. Standing in the area of the platform that he had noted was a dead spot for the cameras, he looked forward to the nap he was going to have on the train.

Chapter 7

He loved the countryside and as the train wound its way through the fields heading north he was reminded why. No people. People just made things awkward. When he was on his own he could do things his own way, without any hassle. The empty fields and distant trees, although bare at that time of year, looked so beautiful. It was turning into a pleasant day – blue sky and very few clouds. The sun was bright and high in the sky. If he hadn't known any better he might have thought it was a summer's day.

The previous night's activities played round and round in his mind. The more he thought about it, the more he worried – but not about the actual act of killing – taking that man's life did not bother him in the least. What Cam was thinking about was how it would be seen. Would it be viewed as a hate crime? Some kind of racist attack? Cam hated the thought of being branded a racist. On his travels after leaving the military he had encountered so many different cultures and religions. Remembering the people he met in Malaysia, all of whom were Muslims, brought back such happy memories of good people whom he managed to get to know and work alongside. For some time he had worked on a small island as a diver, living on the beach, listening to the sea at night, eating the local food. It had been one of the only times in his life when he had felt free. With the sun warming his face through the train window, he could almost feel himself back there.

The dead man lying in that house in Birmingham was the start of a battle against the people intent on destroying a peaceful religion and anyone who threatened the free western way of life. There were just as many white terrorists... one of the last terrorist campaigns in the UK was carried out by a white British man, David Copeland – or the 'London Nail-bomber' as he was known. Back in 1999 he had conducted a thirteen-day campaign against the black, Bangladeshi and gay communities in Soho. In all, three nail bombs injured thirty people and killed two, including one pregnant woman. He was eventually captured and given a fifty-year prison sentence. David Copeland had strong ties to the British National Party, and if that son of a bitch was still on the loose he would be right at the top of Cam's list.

One of the United States of America's top ten wanted men was a white US-born man. His name was Adam Gadahn. In 1995, aged seventeen, he started studying Islam. In 1998 he moved to Pakistan, married an Afghanistan refugee and converted to Islam. In the late 1990's he began to support Jihad, and had since become the main interpreter and spokesperson for Al Qa'eda. He became known as Azzam al-Amriki or 'Azzam the American.' He was the first American charged with treason since Tomoya Kawakita was sentenced to death in 1952, for torturing US prisoners during the war. Adam Gadahn was most definitely on his list – but low down. Although an important figure, he would be virtually impossible to track down and find. Cam did not have the resources for a target like that... at least not yet, but one day maybe he would.

The list was endless; inwardly Cam thought of all the expendable people. He knew he could only make a small impact, so he would start with the easiest targets such as Barakat, and work his way up. The process had now started and Cam had to play it through to the end, however it was going to end. He only hoped he would make at least a small difference.

Cam looked around the train carriage, examining the faces of people sitting blissfully unaware of what happened in the background of society. If they only knew what really went on to keep them safe – what monsters were out there. Many terrorist cells operated in the UK, some of them planning suicide attacks. For Cam, profiling suicide bombers was at one point Charlie troop's main focus. That had used to be easy – but then it grew far more complicated. The average suicide bomber was typically a well-educated male in his mid-twenties, usually at college or university.

They were never the mad fanatics people assumed they were. The mad and the crazy couldn't be trusted to carry out their highly-organised missions – they needed level-headed individuals who could be brainwashed and coerced into becoming martyrs for the cause... an easy task if the recruiters picked the right candidates. Eighty percent of suicide bombers had some kind of medical problem, such as limbs already missing or a disease like cancer, leprosy or HIV. Disabilities like that would bar them from entry into the afterlife, but becoming a martyr for the cause would automatically allow them entry into eternal paradise. Those types of people were also used to provide an extra fear factor. Even if you survived a bomb blast, you might have to live with the after-effects of being injured by someone with a terminal disease such as AIDS.

That had all changed, and suicide bombers were no longer easy to profile. They were recruiting people from all backgrounds. A sixteen-year-old female music student blew herself up at a wedding party at which most of the guests were her friends from university. The youngest recorded recruit was an Afghan boy, perhaps only thirteen years old. He was spotted walking towards an Afghan police checkpoint wearing a heavy coat in hot summer weather. As he approached, it was noted he had a big smile on his face; the boy knew he was about to die. After failing to stop when ordered, he was shot dead by a police officer. As he fell to the ground, his eight-year-old brother, hiding only a few yards away, detonated the bomb via remote means.

Now anyone could be a suicide bomber and that makes them virtually impossible to profile. Furthermore, they would become increasingly more difficult to identify as the recruiters became better at their jobs. Maybe it was preferable to be like one of those passengers on the train and not know the truth. Their lives were more straightforward than Cam's.

As the surrounding countryside became more familiar, he knew he was nearly home. The fells of the Lake District came into view and Cam felt the urge to disappear into them. The sensation of isolation that could only be found when walking the hills always helped him clear his head. Maybe he could find time the following day to get out and about before he returned to work.

The train slipped into the station at around two o'clock in the afternoon. Cam had some errands to run in the town, before he could head back to his cottage for a well-earned rest. Grabbing his bags he stepped down from the train on to the platform. The fresh country air filled his nose. Nice to be home.

* * * * * * *

Cam placed his bags in the boot of his car, which had been parked in one of the side streets near the station. One of the benefits of living in that area was that nobody took much notice of what was going on, and they didn't seem to care. He locked the car and walked in the direction of the town centre.

He knew that without the bag he would look less like the man who had left Birmingham earlier that day. He took a slightly longer route into town, making sure he was seen on the town's few cameras. He used a cash machine and did some shopping – anything to show a presence in his home town. Again, he took some cash back at the supermarket checkout; force of habit. Besides, he would need to build up funds for his next outing.

Wondering if his work had been discovered yet, he walked into the Fox and Hounds in the centre of town. Ordering a double whisky, he took a seat in view of the television and waited for the five o'clock news. Cam took every opportunity to watch the news; having no electricity in his house he had no TV and his only link to the outside world was his mobile phone, which he used to access the internet. It was great tool and he could have done with it during the last few days, but he knew he had to leave it at home as it would have been too easy to trace. Cam was amazed at what mobiles could do.

Could it really be that nobody has found the body? He wasn't sure whether to be disappointed or relieved. He finished his drink and got up to leave. Sliding the wooden chair under the table he stepped out on to the street. The sun had begun to set on a winter afternoon, and the streets were full of people making their way home from work. Cam put his hands in his pockets and pulled his collar up around his neck to protect himself from the winter air. As he walked down the road it felt as if the whole town was walking in the opposite direction, and he hunched his shoulders as he wove his way through the throngs of pedestrians. Cam always felt uncomfortable in large groups of people. The glow from the lamp posts, car headlights and the people moving past him seemed to blur together. He never felt more disconnected from society. 'I'm different from all these people,' he thought. 'Not better – just different.'

After ten or fifteen minutes' driving, the car finally started to warm up. 'I wonder if Mr and Mrs Crossley are in?' They normally were. As he pulled into the long driveway he had a good view of the little country cottage. There she was in her usual place in the kitchen. She waved through the steamy glass as Cam locked his car. 'Evening, Mrs Crossley.' Cam waved as he approached his door. She was saying something.

'I'll pop round and see you tomorrow, Mrs Crossley,' Cam mouthed in an exaggerated fashion.

With the door shut behind him he realised he'd left his bags in the boot of his car. 'Sod it!' he thought. He turned and left his house. His local and favourite pub was about two miles' walk away, in the nearest village. He liked the walk – it gave him time to think. Mrs Crossley was still waving as he walked into the darkness. Cam whispered through a clenched smile, 'Crazy old lady!'

His local was a proper old pub – it had that old pub smell, with wooden beams and a faint whiff of old tobacco from former times. Although he was known as a regular, people left him alone and there was just the normal small-talk.

'Hi Cam, how's things?' said John the barman as Cam entered.

'Same old, same old. And you?' Cam replied.

'Can't complain – nobody would listen anyway.'

'I know how that feels.'

'How's work been?' asked John. Cam thought for a second.

'Lost someone last night.'

'Sorry to hear that, mate.'

'Couldn't be helped.'

'What can I get you? Your usual?'

'Let's make it a double.'

As he sipped his fourth double scotch he started to feel the distinct warmth of the alcohol starting to affect him. He'd watched the nine and ten o'clock news and still nothing. He was starting to suspect that something was going on. The body must have been found by now. Anyway, if he was heading for the fells the following day, he knew he had better call it a night. He stumbled off home, thinking through a fuzzy head, 'Why?'

Chapter 8

Cam woke up with the light streaming through his curtains. He looked over at his phone; the screen showed that it was ten past nine. He felt refreshed and relished the prospect of a day out on the fells. The cottage felt cold – he had not had a fire lit in several days, but he wasn't going to waste time fussing over domestic matters. As he collected his walking gear and packed it into a rucksack, he tryed to decide which set of hills to head for.

Downstairs in the kitchen, he cut rough slices from a loaf. He found some sliced ham in the cupboard and sniffed it. Without a fridge all of his fresh food had to be subjected to the sniff-test. It passed, and he slapped some between the slices of bread. He bolted down some cereal, swigged a glass of orange juice and was ready to go.

The small village of Braithwaite, in the middle of the national park, was at the foot of some of the greatest hills in the Lake District. Cam's chosen route took him down Newlands Valley to the base of Causey Pike, then up to the peak, along the ridge and round on to Barrow.

After a couple of hours he sat down among the rocks to eat his sandwiches, taking in the view. He had done the walk many times before, and it was always the scenery, rather than the strenuous ascent, that took his breath away; it never failed to impress him. Causey Pike reared up to his right while the valley lay to his left and in front of him, Derwent Water. A powerful roar broke the peace as two Air Force training jets snaked their way through the valley. Watching them disappear into the distance, Cam felt a twinge of envy.

He hadn't been a star pupil at school. He wasn't unintelligent, but he simply hadn't been academic. He wondered how his life would have turned out had he applied himself. He had many reasons to thank the military; they had made a man out of the boy. It was only when he had begun to gain qualifications in the army that he had realised he had a higher quotient of brain cells than he had imagined.

The next day saw a return to normality with the start of a run of day-shifts. The weary night-crew went home and he checked over the ambulance with Nick. Once the daily checks had been completed they retired to the rest room and waited for a call. Nick talked about his family; he was devoted to them. The ambulance service shift pattern was demanding and probably didn't dovetail too well with family life, Cam thought. As Nick rambled on, Cam nodded, with one eye and ear on the news.

'Incredible… it's like it never happened!' he mused. Cam fully expected to be talking about a murder in Birmingham. Something must be going on; could it be getting covered up? Either by the Intelligence Services, or perhaps by Al Qa'eda? Maybe they think it was some kind of a hit by one of their own – some kind of inside job. The possibilities were endless. In a strange way he felt encouraged by the fact it was being ignored. He wondered if it was too soon to start planning the next one.

The day ground on with nothing serious happening. They went to a call where an old lady had fallen over and couldn't get herself up. She was an MS sufferer, living alone. She'd had to pull herself along the floor into the kitchen and from there she'd phoned for help. She wasn't injured – they'd simply had to get her to her feet and check her over. Cam sensed her loneliness. Jobs like that really got to him – more so than the stressful or traumatic ones. Sometimes he looked at people and it was as if he was holding up a mirror to his own future. The inevitability of old age scared him, whereas hunting down and eliminating a terrorist didn't.

He had to keep the momentum going. In just under two weeks time he had another four days off.

* * * * * * *

It was a wild night; Cam looked out of the window and poured himself a whisky. It was good to have the night off. The cottage was warm and now he had time to relax. Putting the half full glass down on the coffee table, he pulled out the scrabble box from the pile of board games. The heat from the fire warmed the side of his face as he sat on the sofa. He put his feet up on the table and took a sip of whisky. He opened the box and flicked through the files inside, looking for a name – the name of the next man who deserved to die.

Abdul-Waajid Jabara, aged twenty-eight, was a recent inmate of Guantanamo Bay, released by the Americans and returned to his home soil of Bradford. He was released because the US Government had no evidence of his terrorist activities, however, in Cam's documents he had a significant past. He was a known terrorist and a member of Al Qa'eda. Despite being born and raised in the UK, he had decided to turn on his native country. For some reason he had a hatred of the free world – but had no problem living in that freedom. He attended training camps in Pakistan and had his movements monitored in Afghanistan. Cam wondered how many British soldiers had been killed or injured in horrific ways because of him.

But what had mostly made him a target for Cam, was that he was suing the British government for the time he spent in Guantanamo Bay, and for the torture he was subjected to while there. 'Torture – they had no idea!' If, or more likely when, he won, he would receive a million pounds in compensation. 'This country is so weak,' he thought, 'we seem to allow them to walk all over us.' Soldiers lost their limbs and could only expect to get a couple of hundred thousand pounds in compensation. They had to live the rest of their lives with a disability – two hundred thousand wouldn't go far… but fight for the enemy and we are quite happy to reward you.

The more Cam thought about this man, the more his blood boiled. 'Where do they get the nerve to try this shit?! Do they truly believe they are entitled to compensation? What does it matter? I have the chance to put a stop to this.' He would take pleasure in killing Jabara, and in two days time he would have his opportunity.

Chapter 9

The train was full, and Cam was starting to get agitated. Packed in like cattle, he could smell the people around him. He hated that smell – the unwashed hair and body odour that you couldn't get out of your nose, no matter how hard you kept blowing air out of your nostrils. Still, there was only one more hour to go before he arrived in Bradford.

He would have liked another opportunity to read over his notes, but that was not possible. The file stayed in his bag, which he kept at his feet. He had placed his leg through the strap to stop it going missing. He couldn't risk losing that bag.

He was not even allowed the chance to go over things in his mind as the passenger sitting next to him seemed to want to strike up a conversation. He was obviously one of those people who ignored the fact that, no matter how much they kept talking, no one was paying any attention. Random questions and unrelated topics appeared to flow out of him. Although Cam was getting annoyed, he had to admire the man – talking constantly for nearly two hours was quite a feat. Cam wondered if he would be so talkative if he knew the stranger he was irritating had a gun in his bag. As the subject changed again, Cam realised he was now talking about national identity cards.

'Why should we be controlled like that?' the man said. 'It's an invasion of our privacy. Just because the so-called British intelligence service can't keep track of the terrorists, they want to keep us all under surveillance.' Now he had Cam's attention. 'They can't even protect us from home-grown terrorists. How many more times will there be bomb threats or, even worse, another attack like 7/7? They are just incompetent.'

He had touched a nerve then!

'I'm going to stop you there,' Cam said, turning to face the man. He stared into his eyes. 'Are you on Facebook?'

'Yes.'

'What about Twitter? Do you Tweet?' asked Cam, with a hint of sarcasm and anger in his voice.

'Yes I do, sometimes.'

'So, let me get this straight. You are quite happy to put all your personal details on the Internet, update your exact location and what you are doing at every precise moment. However, you're opposed to a simple thing like a national identity card – something that would improve the security of the nation.' The man was at last speechless. Cam picked up his bag and pushed past him. He would prefer to stand for the remaining half an hour.

As the train pulled into Bradford, Cam grabbed his holdall and, his rucksack on his back, he stepped off the train. He'd never been to Bradford before and something in the air of the place – or at least the area where Abdul-Waajid Jabara lived, displeased him.

Those so-called 'no-go areas' in some towns and cities such as Bradford, angered Cam. They no longer resembled British streets; you could just as well be in some other country. There was a startling contrast between this place and Small Heath in Birmingham, where Cam's first job had been. There they promoted the Muslim faith and improved their community, whereas in this part of Bradford they seemed only to want to let it fall into disrepair. He was walking on the outskirts of the suburb where Jabara lived and it looked like a slum or shantytown from some movie. If you were white and were unfortunate enough to live in that part of town, you would have to put up with constant wailing from the many mosques at all times of the day. The local infidels had grown to despise those calls to prayer. If only the Muslim inhabitants could integrate and refrain from being so assertive, perhaps they might be accepted. They appeared to enjoy pushing the buttons of the local people around them, who had to hide their own faith. Anything remotely Christian such as nativity plays and Easter had to be altered to be sensitive to other faiths. You couldn't even fly the Union Flag outside your house in case you happened to offend someone. Cam wondered how political correctness could have turned into such a farce.

Cam would need to move unnoticed at all times when in and around this part of town. Were he to be spotted he would look suspicious – white people were not welcome in that area. The authorities refuted the existence of no-go areas for whites in British cities, but it was plain to see that they were there. Looking around as he circled the derelict buildings, he wondered why any white person would want to go in there. It felt like a war in which they had lost territory. Cam didn't like thinking of it in that way, but he couldn't help it.

He made his way through the back streets towards his accommodation – another small bed-and-breakfast where he could sleep and prepare. He could only enter the target area at night and couldn't risk being seen. So, sleep during the day and work in the hours of darkness.

* * * * * * *

Cam's eyes were shut. He could usually sleep anywhere, but that day, for some reason, it was different. The unknown element of the task was getting to him. Would he even be able to get near to the target's house? He had mapped it out on a street plan, but if there were too many people, he might have to abort the operation altogether.

His bag was packed and ready on the floor at the end of the bed. This time it was heavy – he didn't have the luxury of knowing what would be needed, so he had to carry everything. 'Travel light, move fast' would have to wait for another time.

He looked over at the alarm clock on the bedside cabinet, to check that it was still set for dusk. It only cost one pound, but that little clock had been everywhere with him. He'd had it years and it must have been round the world more than once. It'd travelled more than the average person and seen more war zones than any other bedside companion.

As the hours ticked by he knew he had less and less time for sleep. It was three in the afternoon – only two hours left – and he was still wide awake. Cam tried to clear his mind and relax into the bed. Four o'clock – just one hour left. He tried the old trick of concentrating on relaxing his toes, then his ankles, shins, and knees, each in turn and so on, to see how far he could progress up his body before falling asleep. Looking over at the clock he saw that it was half four. Hardly any point in trying to sleep. Then he sank into a deep slumber.

* * * * * * *

'There will be two teams.' The boss had his commanding voice on, meaning that either it was serious or there were other people watching.

'Buzz and I will be with TFU 1, and Cam and Spike will be with TFU 2.' They had only been in Gloucester for a few hours and they were already preparing to move in. This was unusually fast. Cam had been in the pub when his bleeper had gone off, and that only happened when the real deal was about to happen. Luckily he had only been on his first pint. He ran back from town and entered the team office to find everyone discussing the task that had been handed to them.

A little over a year previously, a man called Richard Reid, a Muslim convert, had tried to blow up an aircraft with a shoe filled with explosives. He had dubbed himself 'Richard Reid, the Shoe Bomber'. As luck would have it he was a bit of a lunatic and didn't have any knowledge of explosives. Amateurs like him posed little or no threat to national security, but unfortunately, though, he had friends who did know what they were doing, and these two individuals had recently come to the attention of the police and Charlie Troop.

'We will travel with our teams to the targets' addresses and, together with the police, enter covertly and arrest the suspects.' 'Simple enough,' Cam thought.

'The reason the police have asked for our assistance,' the boss continued, 'is that both have been known to set booby traps, so we will lead and clear the way for the police. OK, so if there are no questions, be ready to move in thirty minutes.'

What followed was a flurry of activity as people rushed around getting ready. It may have looked from the outside like a confused melée but everyone knew their own part of the plan. Once ready, the individuals grouped together, forming up in teams by the vehicles, ready to go.

As the convoy of undercover police cars snaked its way through Gloucester, Cam was aware of the surreal atmosphere in the car. Easy listening classics played softly as the heavily armed men drove through the streets. Shoulder to shoulder with the other team members, Cam began to feel claustrophobic in all his assault gear. The convoy split as the two separate teams headed towards their assigned targets, Cam watched the others disappearing into the distance.

As soon as they approached their target's address he forgot about the others and focused only on his and Spike's task: get the police in safely, arrest the guy and get out.

The team stacked up on the street corner, the police with their HK 36 rifles on their shoulders, Cam and Spike with their P226 pistols at the ready. Adrenaline running now, the police team-leader gave the signal to move towards the back door. Their movements slow and deliberate so as not to make noise, the team edged in, covering all directions as they reached the rear door to the premises. On closer inspection, the back door appeared to be a double wooden structure secured by a chain and padlock. Spike pointed at the chain and gave a signal to cut. A police officer used a pair of bolt-cutters to shear through the chain. Cam and Spike took hold of one end of the chain each, and moved it slowly through the door handles. They cleared it without a sound and Cam placed it carefully on the floor. Once down, he readied his pistol and reached for the handles.

The door creaked and Cam stopped. He tried to lift the door by its handles, but still it creaked. Two police officers got ready to cover the room inside. Cam opened the door as fast as he could, trying to limit the amount of noise. As soon as it was open Cam knelt down and took aim through his pistol sights. The two officers leaned over the top of him and each swept the room, looking through the night sights of their rifles.

Peering into the darkness, it became apparent that they had entered through the house's shed. Cam clicked down his night-vision goggles and switched them on. The unique sound of NVGs powering up sounded in his ears as a grainy green image formed in front of his eyes. There was a door to the back left-hand side of the shed that led into the house. That was their way in.

Piles of old furniture, rubbish and bicycles blocked their way, all of which needed clearing before they could enter the house. It was a time-consuming process but vital; everything had to be checked for devices. Trip-wires, pressure-mats, infra-red sensors – the list was endless. They had to check for anything that could alert the occupants that they had intruders. Nearly an hour after cutting the chain they were near the door to the house, when unexpectedly it opened.

The light from the corridor blinded Cam and he flicked up his NVGs. The picture he saw would never leave him. There, in the light of the open doorway, stood a little old lady, her husband cowering behind her.

'Can I ask you, just what are you doing?' asked the old lady, as if unconcerned that a group of black-clad, armed men were breaking into and entering her home.

'Um, is this twenty-four Huntley Avenue?' replied Spike.

'No, you want next door. This is number twenty-two.' Cam felt he was among amateurs and a glance at Spike told him that he was feeling the same way. How could they have got it so wrong? He realised straight away that it wasn't the officers' mistake – they had been given the wrong information.

'Fuck this. Follow me!' Spike commanded. The team moved fast behind their new leader. Round to the front of the property they stacked up on the main entrance. Cam did a double check on the door, to make sure that it was twenty-four.

Spike took the small metal battering ram from one of the officers. He was on a mission of his own. With two smashes, the powerful man had the door off its hinges and in they went. With a speed not generally seen in a man his size, he was off up the stairs, and Cam struggled to keep up. A man was silhouetted in one of the upstairs rooms, and he was obviously still half asleep as Spike's huge frame approached him. With a punch reminiscent of a Rocky movie, he flattened the man and put him on his back. Cam thought he saw the man's feet lift off the floor as he fell. Spike stood over the man, looking down as the police finally entered the bizarre scene.

As the bemused police officers cuffed him and began to read him his rights, Cam looked up at Spike.

'Well, I suppose that's one way of doing it.'

* * * * * * *

The bleeping of the alarm clock woke him from his short but deep sleep. 'Christ! I haven't thought about that in a while.' He swung his legs over the side of the bed, sat up and rubbed his eyes. Looking outside he knew it was time.

The streets of Bradford were a world away from his home in the Lakes. At home there was an air of peace and tranquillity, but now a feeling he had not felt in years returned to him: war!

He stuck to the back streets – it was scarier than walking down main streets, but safer. There he found plenty of hiding places – shadowy doorways, bins, skips, boxes. He could disappear there. As he gradually drew closer to where Jabara lived, it became harder to move unnoticed. After hours of what felt like playing hide-and-seek, he started to think that he might not be able to get close enough to survey the house.

As he sat crouched in the shadow of a telegraph pole, he wondered why there were so many people on the streets. It almost seemed like they were on patrol. There was definitely an atmosphere there – it felt as if something was going on.

It was getting towards the early hours of the morning and Cam knew he would have to make his way out and back to the safety of the bed-and-breakfast. Even if he made it to the house for a look, he would still need to get out under the cover of darkness. 'Damn it!' He looked around as if seeking inspiration, but it eluded him.

He was glad he started back when he did; he had only just got out of the area when the sun started rising. Back at his accommodation he sat down to breakfast – another full English. He could get used to that. As he ate he pondered how he could get close enough to get in. He didn't want to give up on the target, but he might be obliged to accept defeat.

After a whole night out in the cold he was ready for a shower and a sleep. He would need his rest if he were to try again that night. He finished his breakfast and went up to his room. He stared out of the window, deep in thought. From this elevated position he could see most of the area where he had been sneaking around during the night. He looked at the buildings and realised that they all shared a distinctive style. Then it hit him – the rooftops!

Chapter 10

The next night was crisp and clear and the moon was full – not the best weather for moving around unnoticed. On the outskirts of the suburb, Cam found a corner shop with an alley alongside. Only just within the cover of the shadows of the alley, Cam climbed up to the roof using the rough brickwork. The gaps between the bricks were large enough that he could get a grip with his fingers and soles of his shoes. Once on the shop roof, he brushed the gritty dust off his hands. Crouching down to keep a low profile, he looked across the rooftops towards the target house. He shifted the weight of the heavy bag on his shoulders and headed towards it.

Cam's progress was slow and he thought he might be up on those roofs for most of the night. He had to move slowly to reduce sound and pick the right route. Going back and forward to find the safest way took time. Looking down over the edge of one building he realised he would have to make a jump from one roof to another. He leapt with all his might, flew over the alleyway and landed on the angled roof of the next house. Once he had a good foothold he leaned forward, almost in a press-up position. Trying not to slide any further down towards the guttering, he inched round to the front of the building. The front of the house had a small wall running the length of the roof. He kept as low as possible as he sneaked along the wall to avoid silhouetting himself on the skyline. If anyone had been looking out of the windows in the houses across the street, they would have seen the outline of a head bobbing along the apex of the roof. He trod carefully to the edge of this building and came to rest in the corner; he leaned on the wall and peered over the top.

From this position he could see down the street where Jabara's house was. The other side of the street was lined with a block of flats; from there he could get a good view of his target's home. He made his way around to the side of the flats; with a small jump he reached the metal bars that ran the length the balconies which gave him a firm hold, and he pulled himself up, hand over hand, struggling under the weight of his bag until he reached the safety of the balcony, one storey above the roof tops of the surrounding houses.

The individual balconies of the flats were separated by low walls about three feet high. He could now move the whole length of the street, just by hopping over the low separating walls.

As he neared the point opposite Jabara's house he paused in the shadows of an empty flat to look down on to his target's home. It was a run-down terraced house – nothing special. No wonder he was trying to sue the government; it looked like the man had no money. The doors were shabby and the old wooden window frames looked as if they had cheap, insubstantial latches – a plus point for Cam. There was some security in the form of an alarm, but the box on the wall might well have been a fake. Like most people who couldn't afford a decent security system, he had probably alarmed only the windows on the lower floor. 'That's how I'll get in, through an upper floor window,' Cam thought. 'Keep it simple – always the best way – means there's as little as possible to go wrong.'

A couple of doors down the street from Jabara's house, he noticed a home was being refurbished – a building site, complete with rubbish-tunnel emptying into a skip, slung from the upper floor. He would use that to get up on to the rooftop on that side of the street, then he could move along the roof and most probably enter the house using a rear window. He would have to get to street level from the third floor to cross the road to the building site. A very narrow alley separated the block of flats he was on from the next. If he was careful, he could lower himself down it, cross the street and in. Easy.

'It's getting late – I'm going to have to leave it for tomorrow, so that I'll have the whole night,' Cam thought. He took one last look down at the house and up and down the street. He needed to check that no one else was watching Jabara's house. The security services might well be interested in the guy, especially as he was trying to get money out of the Government. With what he had planned for him, they should thank him – he was going to save them a million pounds. One million pounds! How could he have the nerve even to try? How could he possibly think he deserved it?

He might have been in Guantanamo Bay, but people aren't put there without evidence. He wouldn't have been working in B&Q and arrested and sent off to Cuba for no reason. He had gone to Pakistan, saying that it was a holiday – however, you didn't go to the war-torn north and settle down for a nice relaxing time on the border with Afghanistan. He had obviously attended a terrorist training camp before he was apprehended.

Apparently he was 'mentally scarred' from the torture he underwent while in Cuba. Pathetic! What he'd gone through would have been nothing compared with what one of our guys would have had to endure when captured by them. Cam remembered the time when two American soldiers were systematically tortured to death over the course of four days. When their bodies where found they were unrecognisable and it took days to identify them. At the same time, news reports featured a group of Iraqi teenagers getting a beating from British soldiers. It was all recorded on a camera phone and somehow found its way to the media. What it didn't show was what those teenagers were doing before the beating. For an entire week British soldiers were demonised – the evil ones – and all the while those American servicemen were going through hell. They didn't even make the national news. Cam intended to make sure the man would get nothing. At least his death would be quick; he wouldn't even know about it… and that was more than he deserved.

Making his way back over the roofs, Cam mentally listed the equipment he would need. Next time he would carry only what he needed for his mission.

* * * * * * *

The next night Cam was back, watching, and waiting. Jabara's house was quiet, and a bluish light was flickering through the living room window; somebody was watching television.

All day Cam had been mentally preparing for the night's events. Could he take another life? Had he not taken enough? Throughout his time with the ambulance service, Cam had seen so many people who should have lived long, healthy lives, but had been cut down by some random accident or circumstance – and there were some who did not even deserve to live… who barely lived what others could recognise as a life, and they lived on. Usually claiming benefits…

Tonight he would make Jabara pay for all he had done, and for what he was currently trying to do. It still burned Cam up inside that the man was going to claim against the British Government for his alleged torture, but now he had to remain calm, cool and clinical. In and out – nobody needed to know. Just like last time.

He inhaled deeply and took in the smells of the local area. Cam remembered visits to his grandmother's house, in an area where the comforting smell of burning fossil fuels permeated the air, but all he could smell that night was a community divided – a community caught between two cultures.

He retraced his route of the previous evening, clambering up to the balconies of the block of flats across the road from his target house. He waited for the lights of one of the flats to go out, for the occupants to turn off their living-room lights, TVs and go to bed. Then, if he was careful he could sneak past unnoticed.

He moved slowly up to the edge of the balcony window so he could just see in. What he saw was a frail old couple watching TV. Did it look like they knew what they were watching? He couldn't tell. To pass the window he could either get down on his belly and kitten-crawl across, or do what was called a 'Commando Cross'. Another expression Cam hated; it seemed so American. He had been shown how to do it by a US Navy SEAL, and he had to admit that it did work.

It meant he could spin past without the unsuspecting couple spotting him. No matter what they had been through in their lives, they were now about to be part of something big – they were just not aware of it yet.

He squatted with his back to the wall, immediately to one side of the sliding door opening on to the balcony. His movement had to be executed as fast and as smoothly as possible. The theory was to cross past the glass door while spinning a full three-hundred-and-sixty degrees, finishing up in the same position on the other side of the door – it was quicker and smoother than simply walking past and had the advantage that as you spun past you could briefly see into the room. That way he could watch for a reaction from the room's occupants.

Cam stretched his leg into the couple's possible field of vision – un-noticed. They were still glued to the television. In one movement he spun across towards the other side of the sliding doors. He glimpsed the couple as he moved. They had no idea he was there. Probably the most exciting thing that would ever happen to them. 'Ignorance is bliss,' Cam thought.

Now at the far side of the run of balconies, he looked down to street level. The alley was very narrow, just over a shoulder's width. Arms outstretched, Cam lowered himself down, bracing his back against the wall with his feet on the opposite side. Taking his full weight on his thighs, he lowered himself towards the ground, then repeated the process, pressing his back against the wall. In no time he was down. The alley was obviously being used as a tip by the local residents and was nearly ankle deep with rubbish, making it difficult to move without making any noise. He lifted his feet high to avoid disturbing the trash. It was then that the most unfortunate piece of bad timing occurred.

Just as he was carefully placing his right foot down through the newspapers and plastic bags, a group of young Asian lads passed the entrance to the alley. A metallic crunch from a discarded can echoed down the length of the passage way.

Cam froze. There was a brief muttering between the lads, then one of them peered into the alley. Cam didn't move. He concentrated on being a shadow. He was no more than four or five metres from the young man, and he was conscious of his own breathing – could hear his heart beating. However, with the back-light of the street it must surely be impossible to see him in the dark passage. Cam felt comfortable once he realised that he was invisible. The group moved off, talking. To Cam it felt as if they were patrolling the neighbourhood.

* * * * * * *

Peering out from the shadows, Cam stared down the street. The left side was empty. To the right the gang of youths was disappearing out of view. Cam looked over the street to the building site, and thought, 'It's now or never.' Leaving the cover of the alley he swiftly walked across the road, trying to look as casual as possible. He felt exposed under the brightness of the street lights. When he arrived at the builder's tunnel he took one last look around. With the coast clear he climbed into the skip and entered the dusty plastic tunnel. On his hands and knees he clambered up to the second floor of the building.

Dusting himself off, he looked over the rooftops to the target's house and quickly moved along the row until he was on Jabara's roof. He carefully climbed over the top to reach the rear of the property. Lying flat, he peered over the guttering and identified the window he would use as his entry point. It had a wide windowsill that looked strong enough to take his weight.

Cam slowly lowered himself over the edge of the roof, feeling for the outer edges of the window as he placed his feet on to the sill. He balanced, crouching on the sill, and slipped his right arm out of the strap of his backpack. He unzipped it and felt around inside for his crowbar, and prised the window open. The wood was old and rotten and splintered easily.

Placing the crowbar back in his bag he put on a pair of latex gloves and worked his fingers into the damaged part of the window-frame. 'Now to see if there's an alarm,' Cam thought. The window slid up without a sound. Cam hunted in his bag for his small blanket and leaning through the window, shook it open and let it flutter to the floor. Cam took off his heavy backpack and lowered it to the blanket on the floor. Stepping through the window on to the carpet, he turned and carefully closed the window. He squatted down and listened. All he could hear was the sound of the television downstairs.

He rummaged in the backpack and took out his silenced pistol and a set of plastic shoe covers. With the bag on his back, shoes covered and pistol in hand he picked up the blanket and re-opened the window. He quickly wiped the sill with the blanket to destroy any footprints, then focused on the job in hand.

'I'm in, and I have all the time in the world. I'll take my time and do it properly.' Slowly, walking heel-to-toe and on the outsides of his feet, he moved towards the door of what seemed to be a bedroom – maybe even Jabara's own room. 'Not a good idea to stay in here,' Cam thought.

He peered out into the landing of the first floor and spotted a built-in wardrobe – he could wait in there. Before moving on to the landing he listened again for movement. Nothing. Only then did he notice the smell. It was the smell of a dirty house, belonging to a slovenly and grubby person – a smell all too familiar to him. In a few careful steps he was in front of the wardrobe. The door opened with a small click – it had probably not been opened in years – and he disappeared inside.

His plan was clear. 'I'll stay in here and wait for him to go to bed, then take him out – just like the last one. If he happens to open this door, I'll make a quick ID of the man, and positively identify him if I can – then I'll double tap him, right here on the landing.' It seemed so simple. All he had to do was wait.

Chapter 11

Cam had his eyes shut; he had been waiting for well over two hours, squatting in the cupboard. He wasn't asleep – he was listening. He found that if he shut his eyes his other senses were heightened. He heard the unmistakable sound of the doorbell – the cheap rasping buzz made Cam's eyes spring open. He saw his plan fly out the window with this unexpected turn. He would have to improvise.

He could hear voices coming from downstairs, but he couldn't tell if they were speaking English or not. Straining his ears, he failed to make anything out, suggesting that they were not UK natives. He could hear only two voices – so just one visitor. But what were they talking about? The conversation seemed to take on an aggressive tone. 'But maybe that's how they speak to each other,' Cam thought. What the hell were they talking about? Their heated debate had gone on for almost an hour when Cam heard some commotion. He could not make out what had happened, but he heard the front door shut and then the sound of one person moving around.

After some pottering around downstairs, that person started up the stairs then stopped outside the wardrobe for a moment before moving on, but to Cam it felt like an hour. He would rather have done the job in the same fashion as last time; kept it clean and simple, with minimal risk. The footsteps disappeared into what Cam assumed was the toilet or bathroom. Cam heard the seat being lifted and the sound of a zip. He was urinating. Was it still Jabara?

With the flush of the toilet the man left the bathroom and entered the bedroom. Cam heard movement around the room, then some heavy fast footsteps growing louder. He was coming back towards the landing!

The cupboard door flew open and the man gasped as he realised someone was hiding inside. Cam was discovered. In an instant he shot to his feet, head-butting the man's chin as he stood up. The unknown man fell to the floor, clutching his face. Cam stepped out of the cupboard and tried to get a look at him to identify him, but the man on the floor swept Cam's feet out from under him, and he fell to the floor. Cam levelled his pistol at his opponent's head. In an involuntary reflex the man removed his hands from his face and placed them behind his back in an attempt to shimmy away from danger.

Cam hesitated – this was not the man he had come for. It was not Jabara. In one smooth movement, Cam rose to his feet without breaking his aim. He stood for a moment, considering his options. The unknown man now had his back to the wall – he had nowhere else to go. Cam could see the hatred in the man's eyes. Even in his desperate situation, the passion for his cause was still evident. Cam took two steps forward, never relaxing his aim. Cam saw no fear in him, only contempt.

The man must have realised that he was about to die. He went to move – to attack Cam – but he was ready and smashed him squarely in the face with the bottom of his foot, knocking him out. Cam could not kill an innocent man. For all he knew he was no more than an acquaintance of Jabara's and had done no wrong. He also knew that the possibility of the man being completely unaware of Jabara's crimes was far from remote, making him guilty by acquaintance. But he would never take the chance.

He knelt down near the man's slumped body. He grabbed him by the hair and lifted it to take a good look at him. He bore absolutely no resemblance to Jabara, however, that was no proof that they were not related. Letting go and standing up, the man rolled on to his side. Cam turned to leave. 'If I exit by the front door I can simply cross the street and be out of here,' he thought.

He unlocked the front door and removed the safety chain. Opening the door he looked up and down the street. It was all clear, and he now had a decision to make. He could cross the street and climb back up to the balconies and go back the way he had come – or he could make a run for it. Mulling it over for a few seconds, Cam chose to run. It was early morning and still quiet. It was safe to go.

Cam closed the door behind him and took to his heels. He would be out of the neighbourhood and back to safety in no time.

* * * * * * *

On the other side of the street, one door down from Jabara's and out of Cam's sight, sat a small, beat-up old transit van. Inside were two men with tired red eyes, looking open-mouthed at a monitor screen. One turned to the other, who continued to stare at the monitor.

'Who the hell was that?'

Chapter 12

The next two days were some of the strangest of Cam's life. The contrast between his two missions was immense. One could not have gone better – the other could not have been worse. Cam puzzled over the identity of the second man. He couldn't risk going back, so he would either have to give up the whole programme or move on to the next target.

Anyway, for now he was home, safe in front of his fire and sipping Johnnie Walker Red Label whisky. This was rare treat; he usually bought himself any whisky that was on sale. Not the cheap crap – he insisted on at least a well-established brand – but he couldn't tell the difference between blended and single malt, so any good blend would do. Today though, he had got himself something he'd never tried before – a very rare treat. Usually he was careful with his money, not only because the ambulance service paid so poorly, but because his money went elsewhere.

The next day he would be back at work – the last place he needed to be. He desperately needed to get his head sorted out. The whisky was doing the trick. He felt warm and relaxed. He would have to force himself to go to bed, to be fully ready for the next day's work. 'Maybe another quick dram first.'

* * * * * *

Cam sat subdued in the waiting room of the ambulance station. So far it had been a quiet day. A busy day might have been easier to handle, despite the fact that he really did need time to think. Nick was busy in the office doing his team-leader jobs and Cam was bored and needed something to do. He decided to get the daily cleaning done.

As he wiped down the yellow handrails in the back of the ambulance, Cam couldn't help but feel his mission was over. He could never risk involving an innocent person. God forbid that he should kill someone who did not deserve it. It was over – and that pissed him off.

From the back of the ambulance Cam heard the bleep of the display screen. He put away the cleaning kit and closed the side door of the ambulance. All other thoughts were put to one side.

'Job!' Cam shouted. He started the garage door opening and pulled out the charging line. Climbing into the driving seat he pressed the 'accept' button then double tapped the 'mobile to incident'.

Reversing back into the garage bay, the atmosphere in the ambulance was tense. The job had turned out to be one that did not warrant an accident and emergency vehicle. Cam had shown annoyance with the people at the scene.

'So,' said Nick. 'What was all that about?' Cam sat at the wheel looking down. 'Shall we go have a chat in the rest room?' he continued.

'Yeah, OK,' They moved into the waiting room and sat down. 'Before you say anything, I know that I shouldn't have said any of that,' said Cam, pre-empting what was about to come. 'I suppose I'm just a little tired of going out to people who don't need us. Losers like that get on my nerves.'

'OK, but we have to respect the lives that people want to live. You have to remember that their standards can be very different from ours. It depends how you are brought up. Things that are fine for them wouldn't be for us – but we have to respect their choices.'

'Yeah, I know you're right, but it's still annoying.'

'I know, Cam, but it's our job,' Nick sighed. 'I don't think that's the whole problem though – is everything all right? You seem preoccupied.'

'I'm, um, in the middle of something that I'm not sure I can finish.'

'Well, you don't have to tell me about it, but if it's going to bother you this much, you have to get it sorted,' Nick said.

'It would probably bring on a load of other problems. I'm not sure it's a good idea.'

'Cam, just sort it out. Whatever needs doing, then go get it done.' After a short silence, Cam replied.

'You're right; it's as good as done.' Nick had unwittingly sealed the fate of Jabara.

That night Cam sat in front of the fire, finishing off the Johnnie Walker. In two days time he would head back to Bradford and finish what he had started. He knew how to get to the target without being seen. He knew the layout of the house. He felt confident he could get in and get it done. That should actually be easier than starting from the beginning, he made a quick plan in his head. He was sure he could finish the job.

* * * * * * *

Back in the rubbish-strewn alleyway, Cam experienced a flash of déjà vu. Once again he was looking at the house of Abdul-Waajid Jabara. The scene was exactly the same, but there was just the one light in the living room. He could picture it – the same room that he escaped through last time, with the television flickering through the dirty smoke-stained net curtains.

The street was clear and he leaned on the wall with his hands in the pockets of his hooded top, one leg crossed over the other. He felt relaxed and calm; he knew what to expect with this one now. With the bedroom window broken into, it would probably be a bad idea to use the same entry point. The last time he saw from the roof that there was probably a back door to the property. If he went for it now, he could get in the rear door and hopefully, because it was still early, the alarm – if any – would not be set. Jabara hadn't set it when his visitor stopped by last time.

One last look to make sure it was all clear, then he moved. Across the street, hands in pockets, head down, making an effort to look inconspicuous, he entered the relative safety of the building-site near to Jabara's house. Instead of climbing the builders' tunnel to the upper floor, he stepped over the rubble towards the back of the old derelict house.

The street at the back of Jabara's – if one could call it a street – was similar to the alley he had just left. Piles of rubbish and household waste littered the gutters.

When he reached Jabara's back door, he stopped and listened. Putting on his latex gloves he contemplated the lock, trying to decide the best way to pick it. As he could not hear any sounds from the front room from where he was at the back of the property, he decided to use his bump key. The bump key was basically a normal house key that had had its teeth filed down to the minimum. The technique was to put some sideways pressure on the drum with the tension-rod from his lock-pick set. Next he inserted the bump key – but not all the way – perhaps one or two clicks from the end. Then, while putting some tension on the rod, he banged the key in with the palm of his hand. The fast movement would usually spring the pins up into the drum and, with the tension rod under pressure, the pins would fall into their housing and the lock would open.

Cam was not surprised when it worked. The only problem with this technique was that the noise of the bump could alert people that something was going on. With the lock beaten and the door open, Cam waited to see if there would be any reaction.

No movement, nothing – and no alarm had been activated. The same process time after time; to Cam it was second nature. Blanket down, shoe-covers on, prep his gun and close the door.

Cam found himself in some kind of kitchen area. He hoped it wasn't used to prepare food in any way. If it was, he probably didn't have to worry about killing the occupant – food poisoning would do that for him. The flooring in the kitchen was solid, making it easy to creep over soundlessly. The only problem was the rubbish and debris that covered the entire floor. Cam picked his way to the door that had been left ajar at the far side of the room.

Through the crack he could see down the corridor to another door that led to the living room. It was the same room that he had used to escape through, less than a week before. He could even remember how the furniture was arranged, as long as it hadn't been changed. No point staying in the kitchen – the man he was after must be sitting in that room, only metres away.

The closer he got to the living room, the more he could see into it… and there he was. Cam could see the back of a cheap cream-coloured sofa and the back of a head just visible. The man was slouched on the stained sofa, with his left arm propped up on the backrest.

He had to make sure that it was Jabara – he couldn't allow the same thing to happen again. From the way the room was laid out, it was going to be virtually impossible to see his face without being seen himself.

With his left hand in the middle of the door, his right hand on the handle, he opened it further. Applying inwards pressure on the middle of the door and upwards force on the door handle, he opened the door millimetre by millimetre. The door was opened as far as it needed to be now. Cam knew that Jabara could not see his shadow. For the moment he was safe in the darkness of the corridor.

'So far so good,' Cam thought. The television was on loud enough that Cam could move around with little chance of being heard. He could now see the whole of the room. He would have to approach the sofa crouching down, avoiding casting a shadow in the light of a standard lamp in the back corner of the room. Keeping low, he sneaked forward, trying to keep a constant eye on the target, in case he moved. He was now in position, right up against the rear of the stinking sofa. 'At least there is no way he can smell me,' he thought.

Cam psyched himself up, preparing to complete the second part of his mission. Only five days ago he would have never thought he would be in this room again. 'OK, I'm ready.'

With his pistol in his right hand he reached up with his left. Fingers spread, only inches from the back of the head of the unidentified man, it was time. Cam gripped the man's hair and clenched his fist. Within a millisecond he had the barrel of his silencer pressed hard against the man's temple.

As he pressed the gun harder into the side of the man's head, he pulled it back, making him grunt with pain. He straightened his back to gain him a small amount of extra height. Leaning over he looked down on the contorted face – Cam was one hundred percent positive. It was Jabara.

Cam let go and stood up and Jabara looked up at the intruder. He inhaled and instinctively tried to slide away from danger. Cam had the pistol levelled directly between Jabara's eyes. Thump! The first shot hit him exactly where he wanted. Jabara's head jerked back. Cam could see from his expression that he was already dead, within an instant.

Thump! The second shot hit him in the jaw, nearly blowing it off.

Cam lowered the pistol, and looked at the lifeless body of a terrorist. Stepping forward he reached down and felt for a pulse. It confirmed what he already knew. He was dead. Cam stowed his pistol in the rucksack and looked around the room. What he was looking for he did not know. Maybe he wanted to know more about the man he had just killed. His attention was drawn to a picture hung on the wall.

He walked over to it and studied the huge framed image. It was a depiction of Muhammad. This struck Cam as strange, as pictures of the prophet Muhammad were widely rejected by Islam. 'This is typical,' Cam thought to himself, 'a man like this knows nothing of his own religion. He probably doesn't even know what he's fighting for.'

He looked up at the picture for several seconds then turned away, shaking his head. It was time to go. Just like the last time, he opened the door and made sure the coast was clear. He wondered how long it would be before this body would be found. He didn't actually know if the last one had been found. He had no idea what was going on there... Then he was out and gone.

* * * * * *

In an undisclosed location, the same two men rewound the black-and-white recording and tried to find the best view of the man they had seen six days previously, finally stopping at a frame of Cam looking straight up into the camera.

A third man, well-dressed, leaned over between the two operators.

'Is that him?'

'Yes,' replied one of them.

The smart man reached between the two surveillance operators and pressed 'stop' on the console, ejected the CD and placed it in his pocket.

'OK, gentlemen, two things. I want to know everything about that man – and I mean everything.' He gave them both a menacing stare. 'Then I want you to forget you ever saw him.'

Chapter 13

The next night Cam was sitting in front of his fire, using his phone to monitor the national news. For the second time nothing appeared. 'Maybe it's not being seen as newsworthy'. But Jabara was trying to sue the government; he would have thought that might have been of interest to someone.

Looking through his files he wondered what to do with the ones relating to the two targets that had been eliminated. 'I should probably get rid of these,' he thought to himself. 'I'll take them out into the countryside tomorrow and burn them.'

Surprisingly, he had not given any thought as to who would be next. He thumbed through his diary, checking his shifts. There would be no chance of getting away from work for at least two weeks. That would give him plenty of time to plan the next one. He closed the files and put them away in the Scrabble box, then picked up his whisky.

Cam woke early the next morning. He had left his curtains open so he would wake up naturally with the sunrise. He had slept very deeply, probably due to the mount of Teacher's he had drunk before turning in. He splashed his face with cold water and stumbled into the living room. Looking over at the couch he noticed the two files that he planned on destroying that day. Cam could not believe that he had left them out in plain view. 'Shit! Felt sure I had put them away.' Walking over to them he tried to picture how he had left them before going to bed. He couldn't remember… He glanced around the rest of the room; he didn't really know what he was looking for, but for some reason he felt paranoid. Shaking it off, he made some breakfast and headed out.

Driving towards Penrith, he took a right and headed for Ullswater. He knew a quiet spot, not frequented by many people; it was also one of his favourite places. The surface of the lake was undisturbed, like glass. Some early morning fog still lingered on the far side, waiting for the sun to burn it off.

The car park at Aira Force waterfalls was almost deserted at that time in the morning. He parked up and with the files tucked under his arm he walked up the path towards the falls. Passing the fallen tree with thousands of coins that had been hammered into it, he wondered absently how much money was there.

Further up the hill he arrived at the small arched stone bridge that crossed over the waterfall. He paused on the bridge and looked down on the water cascading into the pool at the bottom. He could feel the cold spray from the falls rising up and settling on his face. It felt fresh and clean. Some ice still clung to the rocks – a remnant from the cold weather of the previous month. The weather was warming up, but the sun never got to that place.

Continuing up the hill he reached the rocky outcrop which offered a great view of the lake. From there, if you arrived as the sun was going down, you could see a reflection on the lake that looked like a flame rising from the water. Although it was only an optical illusion from the headlights of the cars through the trees, it was still impressive. It was that which had prompted him to choose the place for destroying the files.

Cam cleared some ground behind the rocks and placed the files in the muddy space. He put a match to the corner of one of the files, it took a while to catch but then they began to burn. The files of notes and photos curled up and burnt to grey and black ashes. Once they were fully destroyed and unrecognisable, he stamped out the embers. With the sole of his boot he mixed the ashes into the mud and soon there was nothing left.

Walking back to his car he felt satisfied that there was very little to connect him with the two crimes. He had a rare feeling of being safe and content. Heading down the path lined with bare trees, he thought back to the summer. Back then, when the tree canopies had been full, you could hardly see the river in the valley, but today it was clearly visible through the naked trees.

Cam looked forward to the warm weather returning. 'Everything looks so different in the summer.'

* * * * * * *

Cam pulled up in his driveway and noticed that Mrs Crossley was at her window again. 'Christ! Doesn't she ever leave the kitchen?' Cam got out of his car and locked the doors. Again Mrs Crossley waved and said something. 'She still has no idea that I can't hear her,' he thought. Cam waved back to her as he headed to the pub.

'See you later, Mrs Crossley,' he called, as he walked away.

Approaching the pub Cam saw only one car in the car park, but he expected it to be quiet. On entering he couldn't see anyone in the bar area. He walked over to John.

'Quiet one, John?'

'Certainly is. What can I get for you, the usual?'

'Please. Any specials on for lunch today?'

'There's a good steak and ale pie. How would that be?'

'Sounds great,' he said as he picked up his double grants. 'Cheers.'

'The pie will be about ten or fifteen minutes.'

'That's fine.' Cam picked up a newspaper from the bar. 'Can you stick the news on the box?'

'No problem.'

Cam was sat at his table reading the paper and waiting for his lunch, when he became aware that someone had sat down opposite him. Thinking that it was his food arriving he lowered the newspaper. Cam was surprised to see a smartly dressed, intelligent-looking man staring back at him.

'Hello,' Cam said, with a quizzical edge to his voice. 'Can I help you?' he added.

'That depends, Robert,' the stranger replied, his voice well-spoken. Cam was taken aback by being called Robert. He hadn't been called by his first name in years. At Cam's silence he continued.

'Robert Cameron, aged 34, born in Malta on the fifth of October, 1976. Born into a military family. After school, and two years at college you joined the army. After a few years' service, transferred to the UK Special Forces. There you were part of a team who specialised in covert counter-terrorism, spending most of your time countering the suicide bomber threat on the UK mainland.'

The man paused for breath, assessing Cam's reaction. Cam looked around the pub, making sure there was still no one around.

'Who are you?' Cam said.

'You've spent time in Sierra Leone, Afghanistan and Iraq, among other places,' he continued. 'You are trained to survive and fight in arctic, jungle and desert conditions. You are an expert in all aspects of covert operations, a military diver and parachutist and very good at getting in and out of places undetected. Do I need to continue?'

'No.'

'But, most important of all,' the man continued, 'you don't seem to mind taking the enemy's life!' The stranger leaned forward and rested his elbows on the table, as if he knew that he now had Cam's undivided attention. And he did. Cam could feel that rising feeling – that feeling of panic, like you have just been caught.

It was a feeling that started in the stomach and slowly rose up into the chest, eventually filling the head with irrational thoughts as the face flushed red. But Cam resisted his natural instincts and tried to keep calm; he could not let this man know he had him.

'So you know who I am.' Cam said as the man sat looking him in the eyes. 'But who are you?'

'I am here to ask you what you were doing two days ago.'

'I was out on the hills.'

'Alone?'

'Yes, alone,' Cam replied almost immediately.

'Are you sure you weren't in Bradford? Because I happen to have some rather convincing evidence that says you were there two days ago.' Cam stared back at the confident man.

'What do you want?'

'I want to know why you did what you did.' The man leaned back in his chair.

'And what is it you think I've done?'

'Robert, don't answer a question with a question. We know about Abdul-Waajid Jabara.'

'What do you know about him?' Cam was not sure he wanted to hear the answer to this question.

'We know you killed him.'

'Here you go Cam.' John placed the plate in front of him and waited for a response, but none came. Cam barely acknowledged his presence. John appeared to detect some tension between the two men.

'Is everything all right, Cam?' Eventually Cam responded.

'Yes thanks, John. I'll pay for everything as I leave if that's OK?'

'Yeah, that's fine,' John said and walked away. 'If you need anything, just shout out. I'll be just over there.'

'Thanks, John.'

Cam knew that he was caught and that it was over.

'Are you here to arrest me?' he asked eventually.

'That depends on you,' the suited man mused.

'Depends on me? Who are you with? Police, MI5, who?'

'We are our own entity. Our actions are our own. We answer only to ourselves and we are the only ones who know we exist.'

'I don't really understand what's going on here. If you're not here to arrest me, what are you doing here?'

'Well, Robert, We want you to be one of us.'

'And what if I don't want to be one of you?'

'In that case, you go to prison as a murderer.' As the man finished speaking he tossed a photograph on to the table and slid it over to Cam, stopping it close to his plate. Cam looked down and saw a black and white image of his own face looking back at him.

'So I don't have a choice then?' Cam said, as he turned the photograph face down, hiding the incriminating image.

'Not if you want to stay out of prison, no.'

'Why do you want me? What use am I to you?'

'You have the right expertise and experience for what we do. Your skills in covert insertion and your desire to do whatever it takes to keep the country safe is exactly what we need. People like you are few and far between – and we need all of you.'

'How many of you are there?'

'There's more than you might think, but there's always room for one more.'

Cam looked at the man opposite him. He was well dressed, in a smart suit, late thirties or early forties – difficult to tell. Highly educated and very well spoken. Cam knew that he must be high up in whatever organisation it was.

'You're not an operator. You would stand out like a sore thumb, who are you?' For the first time the man looked slightly uncomfortable. Cam realised he might have hit a nerve with his last comment.

'I'm a handler for our people.' Cam had thought so. Most handlers wished that they were operational in the field, but didn't have the skills to do it.

'What do I call you?'

'You can call me Al.'

* * * * * * *

With the steak and ale pie going cold on the plate, and with John watching just out of earshot from the bar, the conversation went on.

'Before I make a decision, I want to know more about what it is that you guys do.'

'Everything we do – even the name of our organisation – is beyond top secret. You only need to know what your small part of the big picture is.' Al paused to gauge Cam's reaction. Cam said nothing; he wanted to keep at least some control. Realising Cam was not going to speak, Al continued.

'I handle a group of what we call "assets". These assets are weapons. They are used to destroy targets, whatever they might be, covertly and with as little disruption as possible.'

'Who are these assets and what do they do?'

'They are people like you, Robert. They live normal lives, for the most part, but when we need one they are contacted and given their task.'

'And what might the task be?'

'Anything that needs to be done – but you could expect it to be of a similar nature to what you did in Bradford.'

'What if I say no?'

'You would go to prison, and this conversation did not happen.' Al's tone of voice changed now, and became menacing. 'You have to remember, we have you on film leaving the house of Abdul-Waajid Jabara on the night he was murdered. The evidence against you is very incriminating. You either join us and help protect your country, or I'll destroy your life. At the very least you will go to prison and never get out. Nobody will believe you if you try to expose us, because who would trust a schizophrenic murderer? Because that's what we would make you into.'

'Doesn't look like I have much choice, do I?'

'No, Robert you do not.'

'So, what do we do next?' Cam asked.

'We send you out on your first job.'

'As soon as that?'

'We don't hang around Robert.' Al regained his more friendly tone.

'OK, what would you have me do?'

'We have a small group of men that need to be "gotten rid of". You don't need to know their names; you don't need to know what they're up to. I will tell you that we have had our eyes on them for some time, and we need to put a stop to their plans. You have complete freedom of movement and can complete the task however you see fit.'

'Are you telling me that I'll be protected from the police if I get caught?'

'No Robert, quite the opposite. We will erase all traces of your movements wherever we can, but if you are caught, we will deny all knowledge of your actions.'

'One of those,' Cam thought, wearily.

'Do I have to cover my tracks?'

'Just make it low-key. Be discreet. We can make some things disappear. We can delete CCTV and your car number plates are marked so you won't be stopped by the police. We'll make sure our guys are in charge of any investigations. Just don't get caught.'

'I'll need some equipment.'

Al leaned forward again. 'What you need, for this job, you will find in the boot of your car when you get home. From then on you can ask for extra kit as and when you need it.'

'When do I go?' Cam asked.

'As soon as possible.' Al replied.

'I'm due at work tomorrow.'

'Don't concern yourself with that – you're going to be ill. I'll take care of it.' Al reached over and took back the upturned photograph, and replaced it with an A5 brown envelope.

'Everything you need to know is here. I will contact you again when you're done. Good luck Robert.'

With that, Al got up from his chair, pulled the bottom of his suit jacket down to straighten out the wrinkles from sitting.

'Al,' Cam stopped him from leaving. 'The only person who calls me Robert is my landlady, I prefer Cam.'

'Don't worry about that. You won't be Robert Cameron for much longer.' John watched as Al left the pub. He went over to where Cam was still sat with the now stone-cold pie.

'Everything OK, Cam? Looked a bit tense over here.'

'Yeah, no problem – just a bit of bad news.'

'Do you want that heated up?'

'If you don't mind.'

Chapter 14

Opening the boot of his car, Cam saw a small black plastic container. He immediately recognised it as a Sig Sauer pistol box. He picked it up and carried it inside. He sat down on the sofa and opened the box. Inside, a new P226 pistol with a full fifteen-round 9 mm magazine stared back at him. It was at this point that it dawned on him that these guys knew everything about him, even down to the type of weapon he was most familiar with.

He removed the pistol from its box, attached the silencer and loaded the magazine. Placing the pistol by his side on the sofa he picked up the envelope and broke the seal. Inside was a full description of the men, their address and their recent movements and habits.

'London!' He lowered the files. 'Christ, the other end of the country.' Taking up the file again he continued reading. It seemed strange to be reading a file like that, that had been made by someone else. He finished reading the whole document and spread each page out on the table. He took his mobile phone and activated the camera function. He snapped a photo of each page then slid the papers back into their envelope.

Adding the file to his own and closing the Scrabble box, he began to plan what he had to do. If he left right away he could be in London by midnight, or one in the morning at the latest. He hastily packed an overnight bag, the same any ordinary visitor to London might pack, with one exception: a loaded pistol.

Taking one last look around his house, he grabbed his wallet and phone then he was in his car heading south. On the M6 he headed out of Cumbria towards Lancashire, away from the hills. As the surrounding land began to flatten out, his mind slipped back to the last time he was in London. It was July the 7th 2005, a date that most people had already forgotten.

* * * * * * *

It was immediately after nine o'clock in the morning. Cam and his troop were on a training exercise near Reading.

'Something's going on in London,' the boss said. 'We have sketchy reports of explosions in more than one location.'

Looks were exchanged around the room, everybody realising that this was about to become a moment that might go down in history.

'We're sending you guys to London and we'll update you en route.' After a flurry of activity the troop was under way. As the news came in it became apparent that London was under attack. There had been several explosions on the underground and a bus had also been hit.

The roads into London were busy and the commuters were all paying attention to the convoy of vehicles heading towards the nation's capital. The words 'Army Bomb Disposal', printed on the side of the vans had the passengers of the cars waving at the men inside. It was the first time Cam had experienced the general population paying compliments to the military. It filled him with pride.

The streets of London were manic, as if mass confusion had taken over. The troop was directed via their radios to move to the Special Forces staging post at Stockwell Underground Station. From there, they moved to the Royal Mail underground line. This was where they would wait – it was a place familiar to Cam and the other members of the troop. They had used it for exercises before, as the line was no longer in use. The military could rehearse for an attack on the underground there, never imagining they would have to put into practice the techniques learned on the real tube system.

By the end of the day the full extent of the day's events had come to light. Four blast sites in all, three on the underground and one on a bus. The death-toll was rising towards fifty and the number of injured reported to be in the hundreds; it was the biggest terrorist attack ever carried out on British soil.

With the intelligence service working furiously, the information came flooding in. Pictures and maps of the blast-sites covered the walls of the tube station. The information was growing as the hours passed. By the next morning, tasks were being allocated to various teams. The intelligence service had identified possible terrorist cells in and around the city – they had been under surveillance for some time, and were watched constantly, but now many were deemed to be a significant threat and needed to be taken out of the equation.

Cam watched the others preparing their missions and moving out, all the time waiting for his task to be given to him, wondering what it would be and where he would be asked to go – but nothing came. The days passed by and Cam remained in the disused station.

The other teams began to return from their missions. Tales of raids against the suspects' homes rattled around the staging post. From Leeds to Aylesbury, explosives were found at most of the locations. Even the car the suspects had used to travel to Luton train station was found, and some controlled explosions were carried out before it was taken away to be examined.

It was about two weeks later, on 21 July, after most of the military had been stood down and only a few remained in the mail station, that the alarm was raised. Another attack was under way. Cam and his team struggled into their remaining assault gear. Shouts of explosions at Shepherd's Bush, Warren Street and Oval tube stations came in as Cam inserted a magazine into his pistol and holstered it.

This was it; there was a strange sense of excitement and fear buzzing around the staging post as the men split into their pre-arranged assault teams. Running to the small mail trains that would transport them quickly into the danger areas, Cam could feel the sweat trickling down his back and soaking into his black coveralls beneath his body armour.

Cam and his team were stacked up and ready to secure their area of operations. It would be a long dash through a tube line tunnel and into the station platform, and they would then make the area safe. The excitement mounted, the adrenaline built up – he could hear it ringing in his ears.

Cam was preparing himself for the sprint; in the respirator it would be hard going, as it seriously restricted the breathing. The lead man had his hand on the fire-door handle, ready to push it down on the command of, 'Go, go, go!' Then the radio broke its silence.

* * * * * *

'Stand down, stand down,' the radio crackled. Although the teams heard the instruction, nobody moved. Then it dawned on everyone at the same time. The disappointment was obvious, the weapons were lowered and the gas masks ripped off. The members of the team took in the cool air, looked at each other and started to walk back to the staging post.

The men gathered around the command post, they wanted to know what had happened.

As they waited for word, Cam could feel the cold sweat beginning to dry on his back.

'There have been a number of small explosions in several underground stations, and a possible one on a bus.' The disappointment on the troop's faces was evident. 'We are exploring the possibility that this is a copycat of the first attack. At first glance it looks amateurish and quite ineffective. At this time the police and MI5 have it contained.'

The men turned their backs on the ops officer and began to return to where they had spent the last two weeks. For Cam it was his hammock, which he had strung up in a closed-off stairwell.

'At this time we are to stand down,' the ops officer shouted after the disappearing men. 'We are looking at clearing this location and returning you to base tomorrow.'

If Cam had got used to one thing it was disappointment. The job was full of it. Many times he had been stood by, ready to do whatever the job entailed, followed by a massive let-down. This time it had been an important one – perhaps his chance to take part in a little bit of history.

The next day they packed their equipment away. They had been released to return to base, and Cam was annoyed he had not taken part. Almost everyone else had been involved; he felt left out.

For the first time in two weeks Cam was in his civilian clothes. It felt strange to be dressed as a civilian again. The returning of the black coveralls and equipment to the metal containers always symbolised the end of the op. As the guys were loading the equipment boxes into their sprinter van, the ops officer came running over.

'We have a situation developing!' he shouted across the station. 'MI5 have an unidentified man under surveillance.' Breathing hard, the ops officer approached the partially loaded van. 'He's on the move towards Stockwell tube station. Potential suicide bomber, get going!'

Cam and Swanny jumped into the cab of the vehicle and scrambled for their weapons. Cam opened the weapon cabinet while Swanny grabbed his pre-packed equipment in a small backpack. Before they knew it they where running towards the fire-door where they had stood by the previous day.

Cam slammed the handle down and the door flew open. They could now see the platform of Stockwell Station in the distance. A train was at the platform and there were people everywhere. The two men ran full out towards the lit-up area. It was as they approached the light that they heard gunshots ring out. Cam counted seven, but some may have been echoes.

Swanny summoned an extra burst of energy and accelerated towards the stationary train and Cam kept up with him.

'Stand down, stand down.' Again, the instruction came through their earpieces to stop all actions. The two men slowed to a standstill and, from just inside the shadows of the tube tunnel and out of view of the public, they watched the chaos.

People ran out of the train, which still had its doors open. The shouting and panic of the train passengers erupted like a volcano. Cam and Swanny didn't know whether to approach and help out or follow orders and back off. They had no idea what had happened, but they suspected the bomber had been taken out by plain-clothes police officers.

They decided to back off and find out what was going on from the ops officer.

As it turned out, the man had been shot dead by the police. He had been seen leaving a block of flats in South London that was under surveillance, and although he was unknown to the police, he was wearing a large puffa jacket on a warm summer day. This alerted the police and they followed him. He had taken a bus to Stockwell tube station and when challenged by police, he ran. What happened next was inevitable.

After the final disappointment of the operation, the team left the city and drove the long way out through south London. They wanted to have a look at the block of flats that the dead man had left. As they passed the block in Tulse Hill, they wondered if they would be ordered back to assault the flat that was being watched. And with that thought in Cam's head they left London. It was over.

* * * * * * *

Now, back in his car, he found himself only an hour from London. The journey had gone faster than he had anticipated. Maybe this guy Al was giving him an opportunity to complete what he was not allowed to finish on his own. He might be able to do what he had been planning all along – but with the help of the government. Cam knew that Al was under the impression that he had complete control of him, and Cam was quite happy to be continuing his work. This new task seemed very familiar to Cam – he was on his way to south London.

Chapter 15

Cam parked up a few streets away from the address Al had given him. He double-checked it by looking at the photo of the documents on his phone. Once he had confirmed he was in the right place, he got out of the car and locked it. He put the keys into his pocket and tucked his pistol down the back of his trouser waistband.

It always felt warmer in London, although he felt he was getting used to the northern weather. It had been years since they had driven past that block of flats on their way back from the London underground, but they still looked exactly the same. It was now two in the morning and the block looked fast asleep. Only a few lights were on, in flats that housed people getting up early to start work. He wondered just how many of the occupants did work. Cam stood on the opposite side of the street where he had a view of all the flats. The one he was interested in was on the third floor.

He looked around. He knew it must still be under surveillance by the intelligence service, but where they could be was anyone's guess – possibly in one of the random vehicles parked along the street, or maybe in another flat that overlooked the one they were watching. They might even have occupied the flat next door, and have drilled through the wall and placed covert bugs and cameras to observe the targets. They must have been briefed that he was now involved and what he was about to do.

'Could this be a trap? Why?' he thought. Al could simply have had him arrested after the last job. Al might simply be using him to get rid of a problem that they couldn't solve. If that was the case, he would be arrested for murder shortly afterwards. If he got away he would know it was all for real. Cam knew that he had to get it done, no matter what.

Slowly the hours passed. The sun would be rising soon. Because of their religion they would be required to get up and pray at sunrise, and this would be the perfect time to strike. Cam waited, then he saw the lights flicker on through the closed curtains. Cam started towards the front entrance and up the stairs to the third floor.

The smell of stale urine burned in Cam's nose as he climbed to the entrance to the long balcony that led to all the flats' front doors. He moved along the balcony to the front door of the flat in question. He paused and listened – he could hear only the faint murmurs of the men praying.

Now would be the best time, but he couldn't bring himself to do it. The disrespect of killing men as they prayed was too much. He would wait until they were done. Cam drew his pistol and knelt down; he carefully nudged opened the letterbox with the barrel of his pistol.

He could see no movement, but a light was on in what he presumed to be the living room. He could now hear the murmurs of Morning Prayer. Even then, although not bound by the rules of engagement, he felt it would be wrong to strike. He could wait.

To his left he heard a click – one of the occupants of the flats was unlocking their door. Cam sat still in the low light of the shared balcony. The door opened and a middle-aged man stepped out of the doorway.

Cam remained still, looking at the man out of the corner of his eye. He knew that any movement would give him away – even the slightest movement of his head might draw the man's attention.

The man fumbled for his keys as he turned to face his front door. Cam didn't even want to breathe – it would form a cloud in the cold early morning air. The man locked his door and turned his back to Cam, who was still kneeling down in the half shadows with his pistol holding the letterbox open. He watched the man disappear down the stairs, and then returned his attention to the interior of the flat.

Without warning, a figure came out the lit-up room and walked away from the front door. Cam had not expected that and nearly withdrew his pistol, however, he fought the urge as it would have made the metal flap slap shut. He watched the back of the person walk into the far room, and as the light went on it was evident that that was the kitchen. Two more people followed him into the kitchen shortly after.

All three of his targets were now in the same room. Prayer time was over, and all he needed now was a distraction.

Cam shuffled to his left and from that angle he could see part of the living room in which the prayers had taken place. It was now in darkness as the light had been turned off, but he could see the corner of an ornamental mirror hanging on the wall. Taking aim at the bottom corner of the mirror he fired his gun. The dull thump of the pistol was almost inaudible, but it was followed a split second later by the smashing of the mirror as it shattered and crashed to the floor in pieces.

Cam carefully withdrew his pistol and let the letterbox close silently. Next came the thundering of footsteps towards the door. Cam stood up and waited, aiming at head height in the middle of the door. If it should open, he would take out whoever opened it, then deal with the others. But it didn't open – he never expected it to. They couldn't have heard the shot from the kitchen area – all they would have heard was the mirror breaking.

Cam waited a few seconds until he heard voices coming from the living room. The light came back on, and he knew it was time. He raised his foot and kicked the door as hard as he could. The flimsy door swung inwards and bounced off the corridor wall. Cam placed his foot firmly on the floor near the doors hinges, stopping it from flying back towards him. The light of the living room illuminated three perfect targets. He took aim on the first.

Thump – the first man crumpled to the floor. Thump – the second followed. By this time the third man had turned towards the front door, only to see the black shadowy figure shift his sights in his direction. Before he had a chance to react – thump. Hit in the side of the face he fell backwards hitting the wall where the mirror had once been.

Cam paused for a couple of seconds, checking for movement. None of them moved. He stepped into the flat and closed the damaged front door. He looked down at the first man, leaned over and felt for a pulse. Nothing – he was dead – as expected. The way he had fallen showed that – he just dropped like a sack of meat, making no effort to cushion the fall. The second man the same. He stood up, and, stepping over his second victim he squatted down next to the third. Feeling for a pulse on this awkwardly positioned body, he felt something – he detected a slight pulse. Unacceptable, he thought. He stood up, aimed at the already disfigured head and fired a second fatal shot. Looking down on the now shattered head, he didn't need to check again.

The man was definitely dead.

After flicking out the lights with the barrel of his pistol, he left the darkened apartment. Closing the door, which was hanging tenuously by its hinges, he exited the block of flats and calmly walked back to his car.

Chapter 16

'I have to admit you have a unique style,' Al said, as Cam opened his front door. 'Unique but effective,' he continued, as he walked into the house.

'Come on in,' Cam said as Al pushed past him into the living room.

Cam had only been back a few hours and the day was turning into a beautiful Cumbrian evening. He was hoping to have a long night's sleep before returning to work the following morning, but Al had turned up out of the blue.

'That was good work this morning – nice to see that you don't hang around.'

'So, what happens next?' Cam asked.

'Well, you're one of us now.'

'Was that a test, or something?'

'Kind of. Anyway, if it was, you passed.' Al moved over to Cam's bookcase.

'You definitely won't need any of these any more.' Al said as he picked up the Scrabble box and opened it. 'I'll keep hold of these, if you don't mind.' Al put down the now empty box.

'This is for you.' Al handed Cam a mobile phone. 'This phone is a link between the two of us. It is completely untraceable to anyone apart from us. It is entirely secure. Use it only for Asset business, nothing else.' Cam looked at the phone as Al continued. 'If I want to contact you, I'll do it through this phone. Give the number to no one else, so if it rings or you get a text it will be from me. All information on tasks will arrive via email. Delete them once complete.' Al handed the phone over to Cam. 'One thing Robert – and this is most important. Do not lose this phone!'

'OK, no problem. One thing for you though,' Cam replied. 'I told you last time, I don't like Robert – I'm known as Cam.'

'Yes, I need to talk to you about that as well – shall we sit?'

'Yes, make yourself at home,' Cam replied.

'Thank you.' Al sat down, oblivious to Cam's sarcasm. 'We give our assets new identities; this helps them to start a new life if they want to. We try to make it as simple as possible for you, and as you answer mostly to Cam, we have decided to move your last name to your first name and give you a new surname.'

'What will my surname be?'

'Sterling,' Al replied, taking an envelope from his pocket and rummaging through the contents. He pulled out a driving licence and handed it to Cam.

'Cameron Sterling! Sounds made up.'

'Well, it is!' Al handed him the envelope. 'Everything you need is in there, including the keys to your new apartment.'

'What?'

'We're moving you to Edinburgh; you're going to be our Northern Asset. The address is on the driving licence and some other documents.'

'But I live here – I have a job. I can't just leave.'

'As far as your colleagues are aware, you were visiting your parents in Newcastle and you had a car accident. You're rather unwell and will not be returning to work. You can't go back. That part of your life is over.'

Cam sat for a few seconds, absorbing the information.

'What do I do when I get to Edinburgh?'

'Whatever you want. You can get a job or you can take a monthly payment from us. It's not much but you can live well off it. All your bills will be paid, your rent, your utility bills, phone – things like that will all be taken care of. And then there's this.' Al handed him a credit card. Cam looked at the card and noted the name. Mr C Sterling. 'This is for asset use only – it will be monitored. We know what you do with your money and this card will not be used for that.' Al looked at Cam. He was no longer surprised; he had come to accept that they knew everything.

'Are we clear?'

'Yes.'

'When we need you, you will be contacted,' said Al as he stood up. 'Remember, keep it discreet and stay under the radar. If you require any equipment for a task, use the phone to request it, and we will deposit the items in the boot of your car.' Cam followed him to the front door.

'After today you won't see much of me, but that doesn't mean that I am not watching you.' Al stepped outside and turned to face Cam. 'Goodbye Mr Sterling, get moving as soon as possible and I'll be in contact.' With that he turned and left.

* * * * * * *

'That's a shame Robert; I will miss our little chats,' Mrs Crossley said as she held up a plate of biscuits. 'Would you like one?' Cam didn't. He was never a fan of chocolate, and only out of politeness did he reach over and take one.

'When is it you'll be leaving?'

'Right away, I'm afraid.' Cam replied.

'Oh no, so soon? I'll have to get you your deposit back.' Mrs Crossley made a move to stand up, but Cam leaned forward putting down his tea.

'It's OK Mrs Crossley, I'm not giving you a month's notice so you can keep it. It's yours.'

'Nonsense, I'll go and get it.' She got shakily to her feet and disappeared into another room to find the money.

Cam sat in the silence of the elderly couple's home. He looked around as he puts the unwanted biscuit into his pocket. The house was decorated in the typical elderly style: patterned wallpaper, ornaments cluttering up the shelves and far too many photographs adorned the walls. Many of the pictures showed Mr and Mrs Crossley in their younger days. If you looked at them in the correct order you could watch them grow old together. Cam liked the thought that they had shared a happy life together.

'Here you are Robert, four hundred pounds.' She handed over a handful of notes.

'You should really keep this, in case you don't get someone to move in straight away,' Cam said as he took the money from the old lady.

'It's all right.' She said again. 'We had this place paid off years ago; we don't need anyone to move in. We always take our time finding a tenant, someone who will look after the place. Mr Crossley's getting too old to be fixing it up.'

'How is Mr Crossley, I haven't seen him in a while?'

'He's keeping busy. He had to fix the letterbox yesterday; the paper boy broke the flap off as he pushed the paper through. But it's all fixed now. He was out all day the other day buying a new whirligig, because the wind snapped our old one.'

'If there's anything I can do before I go, you only need to ask.'

'That's very kind of you, but Mr Crossley likes to do everything himself.'

Cam folded the deposit money in half and put it into his pocket alongside the discarded biscuit.

'You shouldn't keep this much money lying around, it's dangerous.'

'I know, but I don't really have much to do with the bank account, Mr Crossley looks after all that. And we just seem to be keeping it hidden away here at the moment. I'm sure he'll get round to it'.

'Well just make sure it's safe,' Cam said as he stood up to leave.

'We will miss you Robert,' Mrs Crossley said, giving Cam a big hug.

'Thank you for letting me stay. I've really enjoyed living here.'

'You can come back any time; your cottage will probably stay empty for a while.'

'Thank you,' he repeated, and turned to walk down the passageway.

He suddenly felt sad that he hadn't been round to visit more often. She was a lovely old lady, full of stories and always fancied a chat. About to open the front door he noticed the letterbox flap was missing. Looking down he saw it lying on the floor, as if it had fallen off and been pushed to the wall by the action of the door opening. He nearly leaned down to pick it up, but something stopped him.

It dawned on him that in all the time he had lived here – nearly a year and a half – he may not have ever seen or met Mr Crossley. It just felt like he had. She talked about him so much and there were so many photos of him that he knew what he looked like. Cam searched his entire memory of the place and the few visits he'd made. And it was true; he had never seen the man. He turned to see the frail old lady slowly following him down the corridor, and he saw the sadness of loss in her eyes for the first time.

'Good bye, Mrs Crossley.' He said, feeling terrible.

'Goodbye Robert,' she replied. With an awful feeling of selfishness he left the old lady's house.

He was walking down the path that would take him round to his cottage, when he spotted something out of the corner of his eye – an old whirligig washing line, battered and bent by the strong winds. Still there, but damaged beyond use. It made him stop and stand still.

He looked back over to the front door he has just left. Mrs Crossley was still there.

'Will you say hello to Mr Crossley for me?' he called.

'I will, Robert,' she said as she smiled and waved. But Cam knew that what she meant was, 'I wish I could'.

Chapter 17

Edinburgh was one of his favourite cities. He wondered if Al knew that. Off the main high street, Cam's car bumped over the cobbled roads. His sat nav signalled that he had arrived at his destination. He was surprised to see a relatively new building, although still in keeping with the look of the old town.

He drove his car down into the underground car park and found an empty space. Suspiciously Cam stood in the cold car park. Something didn't seem right, he just didn't know what. Opening the boot of the car he picked up his backpack and slung it over his shoulders. He then lifted up the floor of the boot space; this revealed the spare wheel compartment where he had concealed his pistol. With the weapon tucked in the waistband of his trousers, he walked towards the door marked 'Entrance'.

The keys from the envelope that Al had given him opened the door that led to the stairwell. It was quiet, and the carpeted floor made the place feel homely. The smell of fresh paint followed Cam as he ascended the flight of stairs towards number six, his new home.

The front door looked strong and above it he observed a very well-hidden camera. Was somebody watching him? He pulled out his pistol and inserted the key. The door opened and he slid inside and closed the door behind him. He found himself in a good-sized open-plan flat. It was well decorated and modern, clean and new. Cam was impressed, he liked what he saw. 'I could live here,' he thought.

After checking out the other rooms he felt more at ease. The two bedrooms were also well decorated and furnished, so Cam did not need to purchase anything – it was all there. He even had a large flat-screen television on the wall. Connected up to it were an Xbox and an Xbox Kinnect. He was not used to that; his last place didn't even have electricity. An ample couch faced the television; Cam sank down into it with a sigh. 'By God that's comfortable.'

He picked up the remote and clicked the big screen into life. He didn't know that so many channels existed. He pressed the CCTV button on the remote and the hallway of the block appeared on the screen. 'Handy.' Pressing the channel up and down button revealed even more hidden camera views. The car park, entrance-way and various views of the streets surrounding his apartment were all covered. 'Very handy.'

He stood up to continue the search of his new place. A laptop sat on a computer desk in one corner of the room. Surrounding the laptop were other pieces of computer-related equipment such as printers and scanners. Cam would have to fathom out how these worked later. He opened up the laptop and pressed the 'on' button. The computer booted up within seconds, indicating that it was top of the range. Cam was surprised to see a screen asking for a password. He'd figure that out later too.

'A shower! Thank God.' Cam had not had a good shower for longer than he cared to remember. Mrs Crossley's old cottage only had a bath, and hot water was hard to come by. He felt like a caveman transported into the future. Clean sparkling black tiles surrounded him as he stood in the large bathroom. A huge gleaming sink and a large mirror finished off the room perfectly. As he left the bathroom a set of double doors caught his eye. Something looked odd about them. He opened the doors to discover an empty cupboard space. Still something was strange about the cupboard but he couldn't put his finger on it.

His phone rang. He took it out of his pocket, this was the new phone Al had given him and it was the first time it had rung. A number was displayed on the screen, but Cam didn't recognise it.

'Hello.'

'What do you think of the apartment? Nice isn't it?'

'Very nice. It's going to take quite a bit of getting used to.'

'Well enjoy it – everything you need is there, and if it isn't let me know and we will get it to you.'

'The boot of my car, right?'

'Yes… a few other things, though. The password to your laptop is the same as your bank pin number.'

'How do you know what that is?' Cam said.

'We know everything, Cam. That same account will be where we pay your allowance into. Remember the credit card is for asset business only. We will be in contact when we need you and if you need me, ring the number that I am calling you from now. I recommend you save it into your phone book in your mobile. When you call it ask for Al, and you will be connected to me. Is that clear?'

'Yes, how long before you contact me again?'

'Who knows? One day, maybe one month. Just sit tight and stay off the radar, OK?'

'Sure, no problem.'

'Oh, and check out the cupboard in the corridor. There's a false wall at the back.' And with that the line went dead.

Cam saved the number under 'Al' and put the phone into his pocket as he opened the cupboard door again. It was at that point he realised what was wrong with the cupboard. Where it was placed in the wall it had no room space behind it. Cam was right; a well-hidden false door opened into a room. Cam felt the edge of the wall for a light switch. On finding it he lit up the room.

'Wow!' Cam muttered to himself.

What he saw was like something out of a James Bond film: an equipment room, with everything he could ever need – clothing, equipment and weapons. Picking up a HK G36, he pulled back the bolt and looked inside the breach. It was clean as a whistle and probably never used. He put it into his shoulder and looked through the various sights.

'Cool,' he said aloud. He put it back in the rack next to some kind of bullpup sniper rifle. He added his P226 to the collection and left the room. 'I'll have a good look around that later. But first, a shower.'

Cam had what might have been the longest shower in history. He stood under the strong, hot flow, letting the water course over his body. He anticipated a chill in the tiled bathroom floor, but it was as warm as the wooden flooring elsewhere in the apartment.

'Under-floor heating! I love this place!'

* * * * * * *

How do you fill your time? Cam had never had to do that before. He had spent the previous four days watching television, playing with the Xbox and surfing the internet – all things he couldn't do before. After checking his bank balance it was clear that he was going to be able to live quite comfortably off the money from Al.

The money from Mrs Crossley had been burning a hole in his pocket. He was going to go out and make it disappear. It would be the first time that he had left the new apartment since he had begun the wait to be called.

With the money gone, he wandered up and down Princes Street. He couldn't help but check his phone every few minutes, in case it had somehow been set on silent. He needed to calm down. He had bought himself some new games, some food supplies and a healthy supply of whisky.

Princes Street was, as usual, very busy with people going about their daily business. Cam always felt out of place in big crowds; he felt as if he didn't belong in the city – he was neither a local, nor a tourist nor worked there – he was completely isolated from everyone. He stopped and looked over at Edinburgh Castle – an impressive monument. He would like to have another look around it; he had visited it years ago. Cam wanted to lose himself for a few hours in the history of the place but the present was nagging him. All he wanted to do was get back to the quiet of his apartment. He was still waiting.

On arrival back in his flat he put away his shopping and flopped down on the couch, closing his eyes and enjoying the peace and quiet after the hustle and bustle of the high street. He took the mobile from his pocket and placed it on the table next to the sofa, checking one more time to see if it was on a loud setting. It was.

After a few hours he awoke, jerking upright he instantly reached for the mobile phone on the table. Had it rung? Something had woken him from the deep sleep that had snuck up on him. The phone screen remained blank. He breathed out a sigh and finding the phone charger he plugged it into the wall. The phone acknowledged the fact that it was receiving power and then faded to black again.

Cam wondered if he should phone Al or some other number. He worried that the phone wasn't working. He stood up and stretched his back, easing out the knots of tension from sleeping in one position for so long. It was now dark outside; Cam checked the time to find it was early evening. He poured himself a whisky from his newly acquired collection. He chose BNJ, and after helping himself to a generous portion, replaced the bottle next to the others on the kitchen windowsill.

The first sip was always the best; he hadn't had a drink for nearly a week, since he had first met Al back in John's pub. He took another long sip and switched on the television. He chose a light-hearted comedy film and after another shot of whisky he topped up the glass and walked over to the window.

The street was still busy with people milling about. The orange glow of the streetlights gave the outside scene a sense of warmth – although it was almost spring the air temperature was still cold, especially at night. He put down his glass on the windowsill and opened the window. He moved his face closer to the opening and breathed in the cool air. Although a city, Edinburgh still had a fresh feeling, even in the centre.

Picking up the glass he left the window open. The cold air helped him feel at home. He wasn't used to living in a place with central heating. Deciding to check out his equipment room more thoroughly, he opened the false door and entered the dark space.

When the light came on and he had to blink a few times to get his eyes used to the light, bright against the white paintwork. He surveyed his equipment, chose the HK G36 and grabbed the appropriate cleaning kit, then made his way back to the living room. Cam sat cross-legged on the rug which covered a small amount of the living space and laid out the rifle cleaning kit on the floor.

While sipping his whisky, he stripped the rifle down to its component parts. He cleaned the weapon and watched the film on the screen. Between the film and the cleaning, he remembered the times when he had used a rifle like that. He had found it a very good weapon. Probably the weapon the British Army should have had as a standard, but due to some political reason they ended up with the SA80. And after some problems with it they upgraded it to the rifle that was currently in service.

Once it was clean and reassembled he cocked the weapon a few times to allow the oil to coat the working parts. Still sitting on the floor, he leaned back on the couch with the rifle across his lap and finished his drink. Looking at the empty glass he contemplated another. But he was waiting for a call. He had to be careful.

Chapter 18

The monotony of his new life was becoming too much to bear. It was nearly three weeks since he had arrived in Edinburgh. The computer games and technology that surrounded him in his new place had lost their attraction. He was bored; his equipment was sorted out and ready for use, and his weapons were clean.

He had been living off take-away and other junk food – and he was starting too feel it. He had become almost nocturnal, staying up to the early hours and indulging in too much whisky. He would sleep until the afternoon, wake up with a misty head, eat something then begin the whole process again.

Cam hadn't seen another soul for two weeks and had maybe only spoken a couple of sentences – and that was only to himself when something had annoyed him on the news. He needed to get outside, but was nervous of the crowded streets of the bustling city.

It was midweek. Wasn't Wednesday the new Saturday? Cam thought he had heard that somewhere. Maybe tonight would be a good night to try going out. Although the city was always busy, Cam expected it would be a little quieter on a Wednesday.

He stood by the open window, taking in the air. He sipped his whisky as he thought up a plan. From his window he had been watching the groups of people walking in specific directions for weeks. They all tended to go one way in the evenings. He would follow the crowds.

He turned on his big screen television and switched it to the CCTV mode. He flicked through the various images. First he checked the interior corridors then the outside cameras. Everything was quiet. He finished his drink, put on his coat and left the apartment.

Cam followed the small groups of people as they made their way to wherever it was they were going. Cam had no idea where that was but hoped it to be the part of town that was for having a drink. As the young people laughed and enjoyed themselves Cam felt lonely and outcast. He nearly turned around to head home, but something kept him out.

The groups of people slowly joined on to the ends of various queues, which wound their way to the doors of bars, guarded by bouncers. Cam chose one that was shorter than the others. He waited patiently to be allowed in by the gorillas on the door. The queue was full of young kids, all a bit boisterous and full of drunken bravado. And the bar inside wasn't much different.

Cam squeezed himself into a space and waited to be served with a drink. He fingered his wallet which was leaner after paying the small fortune to gain entrance. Glancing around, he could see only the backs of people having a good time. The pack was shunning him; he wasn't welcome there. Five more minutes of blaring music and voices and he had to get out. One of the many drunken morons bumped into him as they pushed their way to the bar, he swallowed his drink and pushed his way back out on to the street.

Cam wanted to get home; as soon as he hit the fresh air he was making his way back – to somewhere that he controlled, where he felt at home, a little bit of sanctuary. He couldn't believe that he paid for what he had just experienced – and so much more than he'd ever have expected. He hastily made his way home.

Back in his apartment with the door locked he calmed down. Here he could wait for his next job and nobody would disturb him. He poured himself another drink and walked over to his window on the world. As more groups of people headed in the direction from which he had just come, he sipped his drink.

The next few days passed with long sleeps during the day, waking with a sore head and red, dry eyes – yet still no call from Al. On the Saturday night he felt as if he should try again. He didn't want to, but after a few lonely drinks he had an urge to be out – to be an ordinary person. He switched on his CCTV and flicked through the various views. All around his building he could see large groups of people milling around, an endless stream of them heading into town.

He prepared himself for going out, all the time thinking about the crowded streets. Checking his phone was on 'loud' and 'vibrate', he slipped it into his pocket and reached for the door handle. But something inside his chest stopped him. He couldn't bring himself to open the door. He reached again for the handle but instead he checked the locks, making sure they were secure. He stepped back from the door. What the hell was happening? He lost his nerve and all he could do was return to the kitchen and pour himself another drink.

Cam's nerve failed him; it was a new feeling. He felt what he could only describe as fear – but a different kind of fear. Of course he had been in far more stressful situations before and had felt scared. But this was different. He felt a paralysing fear of other people – unpredictable people. These were situations that he couldn't control, at least, not in the way he knew how. He would wait for a quieter night.

That quieter night came the next Wednesday. He was watching out of his window and decided that this particular night was the best for heading out. Not too crowded with drunks, but busy enough to be around people. This time he would try to find a place where he didn't have to pay to get in.

But as he watched through his cameras he saw something he didn't like on the screen. A man was hanging around the underground car park. He was leaning against the wall, and looking in the direction of Cam's car. Where he was he would have been hidden from Cam as he approached the car, but he was visible to the camera. Cam watched the man for over an hour, his plan of going out forgotten. During that hour Cam had fetched his pistol from his equipment room. He sat watching, sipping his whisky.

Cam decided that the man was up to something, and he had to check him out – see what his reaction would be to him entering the car park. He picked up the pistol from beside him on the sofa and went to the front door.

With his hand gripping the door handle, he felt the same rising panic he had felt earlier on in the week.

'Pull yourself together!' he mouthed to himself, through clenched teeth. 'Open the door, open the door!' With that, he swung the door open and slid out into the corridor. The door slammed shut and Cam tried to lock it. His hands shook as he inserted the keys and turned the lock until it clicked. With his safe area locked he felt exposed and vulnerable. All he wanted was to be back inside.

His back to the wall, he scraped his way down the corridor, metre by metre. He looked back to find he had only moved a couple of metres from his door, but he couldn't go any further; he was sweating and frozen to the spot.

'Come on, come on!' he said, his eyes darting around warily. His heart rate increased; he felt cold and clammy. He could go no further.

After what felt like an eternity he darted back towards his door. Fumbling for the keys in his pocket he unlocked the door and threw himself inside, slamming the door shut. He clicked the lock closed, sealing himself inside and rushed to his wall-mounted plasma screen. The CCTV image now showed nothing unusual in the car park. The man had gone.

He flicked through the rest of the camera views but to no avail, he was nowhere to be seen. Cam even rushed to the window where he spent most of his time, but still nothing except the groups of youngsters heading out for a good time.

He decided to keep his pistol with him that night; he grabbed his empty glass and poured himself a drink. He thought back to the man he had been called to in Ambleside – the man having a panic attack. Cam had considered the man to be a bit pathetic, but here he was, scared to leave his flat. 'Christ, it's going to be a long night,' he thought.

Chapter 19

Cam awoke with a start. He found himself lying on the sofa, still dressed from the previous night. As he jumped up his pistol fell to the floor; it had been with him all night. The light from the open blinds streamed in and burned his eyes. With the light blinding him and his hung-over head thumping, he pulled his phone from his pocket. Something had woken him up.

The screen was still blank, as usual. He saw as he touched the sensitive screen that the time was quarter past eleven. He put the phone down and heard the noise that must have woken him from his alcohol-fuelled sleep.

Knock, knock, knock; someone was at the door. Cam stood still for a few seconds trying to gather his thoughts. Was this it – what he has been waiting for? He didn't think that was the way he would be contacted. Al said he would call him.

He took a step towards the door then immediately turned and bent down to retrieve the pistol that was still on the floor. He couldn't remember what state he had left it in. Was it loaded, was there one in the chamber? This was not good – dangerous and unprofessional. Cam tilted the pistol over to the left and pulled back the slide just a millimetre or two. Inside the breach he could see a round, seated ready to be fired. He had left it loaded, cocked and with the safety off all night, as he slept with it in a drunken stupor on the sofa.

'Jesus Christ! What the hell am I doing?' he said to himself.

Now armed, he headed towards the door again, only to stop. Knock, knock, knock. Trying to think through the muddled thoughts of his thick head, he fumbled for the television remote and clicked it on to the CCTV camera of his front door.

'Who the hell are you?' Cam thought. The man was unfamiliar to him. The TV clicked as he turned it off.

'Hello,' Cam said, through the slightly opened door. The words bounced around inside his hung-over head. Cam noticed the stranger taking in the chain and his appearance in one sweeping glance.

'Hi, we haven't met but I live on the first floor, number two,' he said in a friendly manner.

Cam stared at the man through his red, bloodshot eyes.

'I was just down in the car park area,' the man continued, 'and I saw that your tyres are flat. That is your car in bay six isn't it?'

'Um, yes it is.' Cam replied, his voice dry and croaky.

The man tilted his head in an attempt to see into the dimly lit flat.

Cam quickly blocked his view by closing the door slightly. The neighbour shuffled nervously from side to side. Cam could see he had made the man uncomfortable. He cleared his throat trying to divert attention away from his prying.

'Well I just thought I'd let you know. See you around.' With that he turned and walked off down the corridor, increasing his speed to put space between himself and his new neighbour.

Cam began to close the door then a thought occurred. 'Try to be polite, you live alongside these people now.' He re-opened the door until the chain stopped it.

'Um, thank you,' he shouted after the man. He closed the door and turned the lock. He leaned with his back against the door and slid down until he was resting on his haunches.

Still holding the pistol, he put his head in his hands and rubbed his temples. From his position on the floor he looked around his living space. What he saw was a mess: kitchen surfaces cluttered with take-away pizza boxes, empty Chinese containers and used Pot Noodle pots. Several empty whisky bottles stood on the floor next to his overflowing bin. Although he couldn't tell, as he hadn't left the flat for some time, he realised that his place must stink.

He rubbed his free hand over his face trying to circulate the blood to his skin. 'I've got to do something about this,' he muttered.

Over the next few hours he blitzed his apartment. The kitchen was de-cluttered, the bin emptied and put outside in the corridor and the empty bottles put into a carrier bag ready to take outside. Once the place looked almost respectable, he collapsed on the couch.

No matter how many pain-killers he swallowed, this headache wouldn't go away. Maybe some fresh air would help. He had to be capable of going out during the daytime; it was different from going out at night. It was crowded social situations that were Cam's problem.

He'd never had to buy so much stuff before – not all in one go. He came home with polish, dusters, air-fresheners, bin bags, washing-up liquid and other cleaning products. Also he'd picked up an electric car-tyre inflator from Halfords; he would check his tyres later.

He popped another two Ibuprofen, hoping to take the edge off his hangover, and looked out of his window. The spring daylight was fading into a beautiful evening. He wondered how the weather was back in the Lakes; he missed the hills. He decided a quick nap might help with the headache and lay down on his couch. Maybe if he was lucky he'd sleep through to the morning.

* * * * * * *

Knock, knock, knock. Cam's eyes shot open. 'Again? What the hell?' He struggled upright wondering what time it was. It was dark outside, but how long had he been asleep? He still had a raging head.

Would it ever go? This time he knew the drill. The remote control was on the arm of the sofa, slotted down the side of the arm-rest was his pistol. One in each hand he turned on his camera. The man looking back at him seemed familiar; it wasn't the guy from earlier.

'Who the hell are you?' Cam whispered. Then the man looked up directly into the camera and raised an eyebrow. Cam's eyes widened. The face looked familiar – it could be the man who had been watching his car the other day, but he wasn't sure. He never was good at faces – something he really had to work on during his days with the troop.

He was always concerned about shooting the wrong person, so anyone with a gun got shot. A crude system but it had worked.

Once again he opened the door with it still on the chain lock. Gun in hand but out of view of the familiar-looking man, he peered through the gap, unsure of what to expect.

'Mr Sterling, Al sent me.' The accent was Irish.

Cam looked at him, not knowing what to do. He was

unprepared. The last thing he expected was to see this Irishman standing outside his flat.

The seconds ticked by like hours.

'Are you going to let me in? Or am I expected to stand here all night?' the stranger asked, his manner friendly.

Thinking through his sore head, Cam began calmly to deliver his orders.

'You're going to step back away from the door and put your hands behind your head, fingers intertwined. When the door is fully open, walk into the middle of the room and stop when I tell you. Understand?' The man nodded slightly while snorting a small laugh through his nose.

'Yes, I got it, just keep yourself calm.'

Cam backed into the kitchen area as the man walked past, his fingers locked behind his head. As soon as the door could be shut he closed it and then raised his pistol to cover the man as he moved into the living area.

'Stop there.' The man moved to turn around. 'No, back towards me. Now who are you and what do you want?'

'I think you're reading too much into this.'

'Who are you and what do you want?' The man sighed.

'My name is not important, and all I need is a place to stay for the night. Al recommended here.'

'Why wasn't I told?'

'Come on, need to know and all that.' Cam understood. It was best not to know if you didn't need to.

'Are you armed?'

'Yep.' Cam now knew he was way out of his league. This man was obviously a veteran of all that was going on and Cam was the new boy. He decided to play it confidently and act as though he knew what he was doing.

'Want a drink?'

'OK, sounds good,' the man said, turning around.

'Take a seat.' Cam motioned towards the stools by the breakfast bar. 'Whisky?' Cam asked.

'Sure, I'm Irish aren't I?'

Cam tried to place his visitor's accent; he was from Ireland – probably southern Ireland, maybe south-west. The man wasn't much taller than Cam but he was stocky and powerfully built. He was dressed in jeans and a t-shirt and hadn't shaved for a couple of days, however, he didn't look scruffy. He sipped the single malt that Cam had given him while his own drink remained untouched.

'Why have I been left here for so long?' Cam finally asked. 'I've been here well over a month and all I'm doing is waiting. What's going on?'

'Oh, right. Now I get it. Look it's normal; after being moved, they leave you for a while. They think that you get so bored and desperate to do something that when you are given a job you'll be really psyched up. You know, and you give it all you've got.'

Cam thought he understood. It was the first time the man had let on he was one of them.

'How long you been with Al's lot?'

'I have no idea what the hell you're talking about. Now, is the spare room through there?'

'Yeah.' With that the man got up. He took a couple of steps in the direction of the spare room, then stopped.

'Look, if you're that keen to get going,' he said without even turning round, 'there's an amusement arcade on Lothian Road. Meet me there tomorrow morning at seven thirty. I'll have a little job for you.' Cam caught a glimpse of a sly smirk as the Irishman walked off into the bedroom.

Cam sat a while listening, but he heard very little from the room. After about half an hour he decided to turn in for the night and see what the next day would bring.

He really didn't want to sleep. He still had his pistol with him. Looking over at his dusty, cheap alarm clock, he saw that it was half four. If anything was going to happen, it would happen now. Cam had been on enough assaults to know that the average person was most tired at around three or four in the morning. That's when he would strike, so he had to be on guard. But that was the last thing he remembered until he woke up.

'Shit!' He scrambled off his bed, picking up the clock. Six twenty. 'Shit!' He opened his bedroom door to see his flat in the same state it was the night before. After searching the entire apartment it would appear that nobody had been there at all. The spare room was even made up, nearly the same as it was before Al's friend had knocked on his door.

The only thing that was out of order was that the front door was unlocked. He couldn't have locked it as he left. After locking the door, Cam put his pistol down on the breakfast bar. Resting his elbows on the bar he released a huge sigh of relief. His headache was gone. Looking out of his window he wondered what he had got himself into.

The next half an hour was a flurry of activity as Cam rushed around the apartment, trying to get himself ready for something he had no idea about. He couldn't risk taking any of his weapons; he could not risk getting caught with them. With a sense of duty in his mind, he managed to ignore the feeling of rising panic at leaving the safety of his flat, and was out the door and on his way to Lothian Road.

* * * * * * *

He reached his destination and there was no sign of the previous night's visitor. The arcade was silent and still locked up. He decided to wait around and see what would happen.

A few people started to pass, probably on their way to work. The tops of the buildings were clear – at least he couldn't see anything with his naked eye, only birds sitting on the edge of the rooftops. At least that meant there was no movement up there, or they would have flown away. He watched as the pedestrians passed with bored, expressionless faces. Cam had never wanted to become one of those people – merely existing, going to work and hating it.

It wasn't long before Cam became aware of sirens in the background. They were hard to hear against the natural noise of the city, but they were most definitely there. To add to the noise, an alarm went off in the arcade behind him. Cam spun around and looked into the arcade but saw very little activity. Feeling nervous he started to cross the road away from the arcade that was now attracting the attention of the passers-by. Before he could cross to safety, a police car came screaming round the corner and headed right toward Cam, who was now standing in the middle of the road. Conspicuous in that position, he remained motionless as the officers threw open their car doors and hurriedly moved toward him. Cam fought the urge to run as the officers ordered him to stand still.

'Sir, can I ask you what you're doing here?' asked one of the police officers.

'I was just walking by and the alarm went off. Nothing to do with me.'

'Sir, we have a report of someone matching your description trying to break in to the premises. Do you have anything to say about why that would be?'

'No, like I said I was just passing.'

'OK Sir; please step over to the vehicle.'

'Wait, I've done nothing here. You can't just arrest me with no reason,' protested Cam.

'I said nothing about arresting you did I, Sir? Please move over to the car. Barry, can you check out the building and try to turn off the alarm.' The younger of the two officers jogged off towards the casino's doorway.

The officer opened the rear doors to the patrol car and motioned Cam inside. He sat down on the edge of the seat leaving his legs outside the car. The policeman seemed distracted; he pressed his earpiece deeper into his ear and struggled to listen to the messages being passed to him. More sirens approached and Cam began to feel that he had been set up. The officer started to look around as if trying to make sense of the messy information streaming into his ear. Then, as if he finally pieced all the parts together he turned and stared at his suspect. Cam knew something was wrong. He had to get out of there. More police were on the way; he had to get away now before it was too late.

Cam forced himself to his feet as the officer reached towards him in an attempt to push him back into the car. Cam swiped the policeman's hand away but he was too strong. The officer was almost a full foot taller than Cam and he was fast with it. He gripped Cam's wrist. Cam knew he was about to be put into a hold he could not get out of. That was how police were trained and they were good at it. Cam had to act fast if he was going to escape.

He snatched at the officer's radio attached to his luminous body armour. He twisted it into an inverted position and released it from its housing. With a flick he threw the radio as far down the street as he could, ripping out the earpiece wire. The officer immediately relaxed his grip and turned to chase his radio. Cam knew he would – those airwave radios were the same as the ones he used in the ambulance service. They were always told, 'break it – but don't lose it!' The officer would rather let his suspect go than face the paperwork generated by loosing his secure radio.

Cam ran for his freedom. He had no idea what was going on but he was sure he was being used as a decoy. It was a setup. At the end of the street he could see more police cars approaching. He disappeared into a side street. More cars sped past the entrance onto the other street casting blue flashing lights that bounced down the narrow alley. Once they had passed out of sight Cam ran across the road. He went from side street to side street, trying to get as far away from his pursuers as possible. Back and forth he went, dodging the ever-increasing police presence, but as the police cordon began to take shape Cam found himself stuck. He could not get out. He spotted a telephone box on the inside corner of the alley he found himself in. He picked up the receiver and made a call he never thought he would.

* * * * * * *

'999 emergency, which service do you require?' said the female voice on the other end of the phone.

'I need an ambulance on Rutland Court Lane, Edinburgh. I've found a man on the ground he's clutching his chest in pain. I think he's having a heart attack.'

'How old is the gentleman?'

'He's mid-thirties, come quick.' Cam hung up before the call-handler could ask any more questions. All he could do now was wait.

Cam hid in the shadows of the alley, hoping the police would let the ambulance through the cordon. After a long fifteen minutes hiding from passing police cars, he saw an ambulance pull up at the entrance to the alley.

It was time to get down on the ground. The two ambulance-crew jumped out of the vehicle and started running towards him.

'Hello there, what do we call you then?' asked one of the crew.

'Tom.'

'Hello, Tom, my name's Craig, and this is Colin,' the paramedic said, motioning towards his colleague. 'Can you tell me what's happened?'

'I was walking back home and had this pain in my chest. I can't walk any more and I can hardly breathe. Some guy found me and called for you,' said Cam, acting breathless and writhing in fake agony.

'Can you describe the pain you're in?' said the paramedic. Cam proceeded to describe the perfect heart attack, straight out of a textbook.

The crew wasted no time in getting Cam into the back of the ambulance. Once inside, the crew hurried around, hooking him up to an array of monitors. He was given an aspirin and a tablet called GTN. Cam had expected all this and he knew it would do him no harm. The technician asked him his age and then waited for the monitor on the wall of the ambulance to print off a heart tracing.

'Looks normal,' the paramedic said, handing it to the technician for a second opinion. 'Are you still in pain, Tom?'

'Yes, feels like something is crushing me.'

'I think we had better get going,' the paramedic said to his crew-mate. 'I'll stay in the back in case we have to give any pain relief.' The technician climbed out the back of the ambulance, got into the front seat and prepared to move off. 'If you had to give the pain a score between one and ten, ten being the worst pain you have ever felt, where would it be?'

'Nine or ten,' Cam said.

'Would you like anything for that pain?'

'No, I can handle it.'

'OK, but if you change your mind let me know. I would, however, like to pop a little needle into your arm, would that be OK?'

'Do what ever you got to do,' Cam said.

As the ambulance wove its way through the streets of Edinburgh the paramedic inserted a cannula into Cam's arm. He knew exactly what was going through the paramedic's mind. His patient, Tom, was mid-thirties with central crushing chest-pain, radiating down his left arm and up into his jaw and teeth. His heart-tracing was normal, however, you can be having a heart attack and it not show on the tracing. This would stop the paramedic administering thrombolytic drugs. Cam would not want those.

He started to relax a little as he realised that they must be well out of the police cordon. Soon he would be at the hospital and he could simply walk out when he got the opportunity. The paramedic asked him questions throughout the journey and was filling out his paper work when they reversed into the Accident and Emergency department of The Royal Infirmary of Edinburgh.

Cam was wheeled into the ward and the crew handed him over to hospital staff. The crew wished him all the best and were off to their next job. Cam watched them go and started to wish he could go back to his old life – back to his old station and the tranquil Lake District. Instead he found himself in an A&E department on a bed in a ward surrounded by drunks and drug addicts, pretending to be having a heart attack.

Doctors and nurses swarmed around him.

'Hello Tom,' said one of the nurses. 'I'm just trying to book you in and the details you gave to the ambulance crew aren't being recognised by our computers. Either they're wrong or you don't exist.' 'This is going too far,' thought Cam. He had to leave. Just as they started to undress him he swung his legs over the side of the bed and sprung to his feet. He pushed through all the hospital staff who tried to stop him. Cam knew they had no power to detain him and he fought his way to the exit and ran off, with the shouts of the nurses ringing behind him.

* * * * * *

Cam arrived back at his place a few hours later. It was a long walk from the hospital, but it gave him time to think. He had no idea what the hell had just happened, except that he had been used as some sort of distraction. He wondered if he would ever see that Irish guy again.

For the first time in weeks his head felt clear; it felt good. He knew it was the result of too much drinking and self-neglect. The events of the past day had shown him that. Safe at home with the door locked he began to contemplate what was going on in his life.

Chapter 20

Over the next few months Cam spent his days running, eating and resting. He felt his body recovering and strengthening, his tissues repairing themselves, through alternating periods of activity and rest.

He found many good runs around the city, surrounded as it was by the Pentland Hills and bounded by the coast at Leith. He was surprised to find so many rural areas. His favourite run was to make his way into Holyrood Park. The park was usually quiet and nobody stared at you as you ran past like they did in city streets. From there he could make his way up Arthur's Seat and look out over the landscape. Arthur's Seat, the main feature of Holyrood Park, had the best panoramic views of Edinburgh. Although only a relatively small hill, he could do shuttle runs up and down the steepest parts of the extinct volcano.

He could feel himself getting fitter and fitter. He almost felt he was getting back to his old self. The eyes that stared back at him were bright and clear; no longer red and bloodshot. He knew he would never get to the same level he was at when he was with the troop; after all he was a lot younger then. But he could try.

If he fancied a shorter run he would go out to Calton Hill or the Royal Botanic Gardens. Every day he could feel the weather changing, the smell of summer in the trees and grass. Everything was turning green and looked alive. This was a beautiful city.

To fill his nights and whenever he was free during the day, he had volunteered as a Community First Responder. These people responded to emergencies and could usually get to incidents before an ambulance, as they were already embedded in the community. He had been made to do the entire responder course as he wanted to remain known as Cam Sterling not Robert. He was nervous about the CRB check bringing up something to do with Al, but it came back OK.

The Scottish Ambulance Service was efficient but constantly run off its feet trying to cover the whole city, so Cam had responded to many incidents and was gaining more experience as a solo responder. Although he was only allowed to do what was in the Community First Responder scope of practice, he still used all the skills he had to help the people he went to.

He was fully occupied and was starting to enjoy his new life in Edinburgh; he felt good and was controlling his drinking – a responder couldn't turn up stinking of whisky.

Now that summer had well and truly arrived, he would usually be found, if not running up Arthur's Seat, sitting on one of the benches in Princes Street Gardens, where he would sit and watch the world go by. It was better than staring out of his window. He would look over at the Burger King from where his undercover exercises were conducted. Or over toward the HMV shop where he would buy his Xbox games that he would sit and play, still waiting to respond.

He would also walk through the park, feeling the warm sun on his face, towards Scott Monument. The park was full of people walking around with ice creams or hot dogs. Students littered the park, lying around on blankets, reading or chatting.

He would climb the steps past the monument – the gardeners had done a great job with the flower beds that year – and walk past the train station on his left. He remembered his initial Army selection course all those years ago. He could picture himself standing with the young scared teenagers gathered outside the station on most days. Looking back he would never had imagined where it would take him.

Cam liked climbing the steep street towards the castle. He would pass all the tourists going in and out of the souvenir shops. Cam liked playing a game with himself, guessing where the tourists came from. Who were the ones with the 'I love Edinburgh' hats or t-shirts on? Or with at least two cameras strung round their neck.

While wandering round the castle he would visit all the rooms and look at the jewels and weaponry. Some of the swords and axes were huge; the men who wielded them must have been massive. He also would try to figure out if there really was a secret tunnel that led out of the castle. Supposedly there was one that led to the queen's palace, a mile away.

Then he would normally rest, leaning on one of the cannons overlooking the city, and enjoy the views. It was there one day, months after he had arrived in Edinburgh, that he heard the phone ring in his trouser pocket.

* * * * * * *

Cam stared at the screen as the phone vibrated in his hand. He should answer it, but something was stopping him. He was happy with his new life; he was left alone and was comfortable. He didn't want it to change – but to keep his new life he would have to pay for it.

'Hello,' he said, after touching the screen and sliding the 'accept call' tab to the bottom of the phone.

'Good morning.' The voice was Al's – at least he thought it was – it had been such a long time since they had last talked. 'We have a task for you. You do not have free actions; you must follow the instructions that are to follow. Are you ready?'

'Yes,' he replied.

'Good luck.'

With that, the phone buzzed once again. An email had arrived. Within the email he found some very brief instructions.

Possible terror act in progress. Proceed to undercover police hub, address to follow. You are to follow strict instructions. Ongoing intelligence updates. Concealed, silenced weapons only. More to follow.

After closing the email he lowered the phone. He knew he probably didn't have time to hang around. He had to get moving. He raised the phone as if expecting more information apart from the little he had just received. A quick glance at the screen showed something odd – something slightly different from normal.

The GPS location app had been activated. Cam always had it disabled as it drained the battery. Someone had activated it remotely. 'I'm being tracked.' He looked up, trying to see through the clouds. After a few seconds he thought to himself, 'What am I doing? If they are watching they must be having a right laugh.' He looked down and glanced around to see if he had initiated any of the gullible tourists into wondering what he was looking at. But nobody was paying him the slightest bit of attention.

It took him less than twenty minutes to get home. He was sweating as he opened his front door. As he made his way towards his weapon cupboard he saw his phone-charger plugged into the wall near the sofa. On the spur of the moment he inserted the charger and flicked on the power.

He grabbed his silenced pistol that had seemed to have been left in his store for weeks now. He had become much less paranoid since he had pulled himself together. He took extra empty magazines and a few boxes of 9 mm ammunition, along with a shoulder style holster that was beside the spare magazines.

Now back in the living space, he knelt down next to his phone, waiting for more information and watching it charge. He loaded the magazines, placing them neatly in the shoulder-holster. The phone vibrated on the floor as he slipped the last magazine into the holster. It was another email.

All it contained was the address of a police hub. It wasn't far away and it would not take long to get there. He left the phone on the floor next to his weapon and ammunition and went to change his clothes. He chose plain-looking trousers and a loose grey hooded top in which he could comfortably hide the pistol and extra ammunition. The phone was almost fully charged, but he had run out of time. He pulled the charger from the phone and placed it in his pocket. With the weaponry concealed tightly around his body, he left his house and made his way through the streets of Edinburgh towards the police hub.

The address that had been given to him turned out to be a large semidetached house on the corner of the road. There were cars and vans parked all over the street and a plain-clothed police officer hanging around the entrance. As he approached the large house he received another email.

Enter the hub; tell the guard you are the MI5 observer.
There will be a mission briefing in the basement. Keep
a low profile talk to no one. Listen to what is going on,
take no notes. More to follow.

He walked confidently towards the police officer who had been given the guard duty. He was obviously disgruntled about being given this responsibility. He would probably prefer to be part of the action.

'Hello mate, I'm the MI5 observer,' Cam said as the officer blocked off the door when he got closer. The police officer nodded his head as he looked him up and down. He moved out of the way and Cam entered the house.

The basement turned out to be a makeshift gymnasium. The room was big – the size of the whole house, maybe more. Amongst the gym equipment undercover police mixed with uniformed officers. Cam placed himself in the corner with a good view of the low stage area.

'OK, listen in, we don't have much time.' A man in high-ranking police uniform had stepped up on the stage and started speaking before he arrived at the centre. He was maybe a commissioner or something like that. Cam didn't know police ranks.

'We have a terrorist operation under way now. As we speak, the intelligence service are watching a cell preparing a suicide attack. They were not expecting it to happen this soon. All intel leads towards the target being the city centre, and within the next couple of hours. So we have been caught off guard. We are moving out of here in ten minutes, so be ready. Snipers, I want you to gain access to the roofs of the centre.' While talking he motioned over to his right, and the sniper team-leader acknowledged with a nod. 'Surveillance, you have been practising for this. You know what you're doing. And firearms, we are going to place you in strategic locations to cover most of the city. Mobile team, take up your position in a taxi rank.'

Cam remembered the armed officers had a hollowed out taxi that could contain a full team. From that black cab they could quickly deploy a team on top of a target almost anywhere.

'And our military counterparts from Charlie troop, you will be vectored in on the target from where you can neutralise the device once the suspect has been either restrained or eliminated.'

Cam gazed over towards where the commissioner was looking to see a group of six guys sitting on some metal containers. 'Shit!' Cam exclaimed to himself. The guys listened to the rest of the briefing, but Cam's mind had blocked out the speaker and he was fully focused on the team on the other side of the gym. 'So, you're my replacements,' he thought. The brief had finished and the six-man team began preparing their equipment. Cam wanted to go over and speak to them, but he was under strict instructions not to make contact with anyone.

He waited and watched as the new version of the troop prepped their radios and slung their day-sacks over their shoulders. This was a strange feeling as he knew exactly what was in those bags. The team talked amongst themselves for a few minutes then headed out of the gym.

Cam walked over to the metal equipment boxes. The only gunmetal grey one interested him. As the rest were all painted green, this one stood out. It used to be his. He stood over the box and looked down at it. There was a stretch of green fabric tape about twenty inches long on the lid. The tape had the name of the owner on it. It was taped, layer over layer, of other name tags. Cam wondered how deep down his name was.

The phone vibrating in his pocket broke him away from his daydream. Another email had arrived. 'Hope it gives me the information I might have missed at the end of the briefing.'

Target area is St James' Shopping Centre. Make your way there and await further orders.

* * * * * *

Before he knew it he was over halfway there – and so many old memories had taken over his mind. They seemed so far distant that he sometimes wondered if he had ever actually experienced them. He didn't even remember leaving the briefing room.

He had to focus, clear his mind and concentrate on the task in hand. It was his first job for Al and he needed to get it right. If anything, he simply wanted to keep hold of his new life.

As he headed towards to shopping centre he prepared by gathering as much information about the area as possible. Using his phone he had found a handy PDF document; it mapped out the centre, showing entrances and exits and marking out all the individual shops. He had opened up Google Maps, showing the exterior roads that led to the centre and its car parks.

The shopping centre was a medium-sized shopping mall situated at the western side of the main street. It was an older-style building, but relatively modern looking inside. Within the centre you could find most types of retail outlets – all the usual ones were all there.

Cam hurriedly made his way south on Broughton Street and recklessly crossed the main road towards the mall. As he entered the mall the phone buzzed, indicating the arrival of another email.

Target spotted at crossroad of Abercromby Place and Albany Street. Stand by. Snipers have eyes on. More to follow.

Cam read the message and checked his mall map. He decided to move towards one of the centre's northern entrances. Stand by! What the hell did they mean by that? Cam knew fine and well that the snipers would never be given permission to open fire. He realised that being inside the shopping centre would not be the best place to be.

Target has turned right on to York Lane. More to follow.

Cam stood at the entrance to the centre and looked out towards the direction from which the target was approaching. He looked up at the roofs of the multi-storey car park and the top of the centre, checking for the snipers – but he could see no trace of them. There were a number of black taxis in the vicinity but none of them were carrying passengers. Had they already been deployed into the centre?

The phone vibrated again. Cam was expecting another email but as he raised the phone he surprised to see it was a call. The screen read, 'unknown number'.

'Hello.'

'We see you have moved outside. Is there a problem?'

'No I'm trying to locate the target on approach. Is this Al?'

'Yes it's me. Move back inside. We will keep you updated on his location.'

'Look Al, what am I expected to do here? I know COBRA will let it happen; I've been in this situation before, so I'm not to keen on going back in there.'

'Cam you are there because we know the probable outcome of this. You are there to stop it happening, to prevent us losing the police and military that are on this operation, also to protect the civilians in the centre.'

'Can I use lethal force?'

'Yes. Now listen, the target has turned right on to York Place. Get back inside and wait in the King's Mall.'

'Moving now,' he said as he ended the call.

As Cam re-entered the mall he took one last look at the people outside the shopping area. One of them is the target. He turned and went inside.

After a minute or so, he was at the centre of the shopping mall and desperate for more information. He dialled the only number on the phone.

'Hello,' said the voice on the other end of the phone.

'I need to speak to Al.' Cam heard a muffled click.

'This is Al.'

'I need info on the target. I need to make a positive ID.'

'We don't have that information yet.'

'What he is wearing, how tall? Anything.'

'We don't have that information yet. Stand by.'

Cam still had the phone to his ear, even though Al had stopped speaking. He had not hung up, merely waiting for more intel to come in from the covert operators. He looked around at the people, happily going about their business. They had no idea what was going on. Cam searched for undercover police, firearms or the troop – but to no avail. They were too good to be spotted.

He frantically looked all around the centre of the mall. It dawned on him that so much time had passed that the target must be inside now. He was running out of time.

* * * * * * *

The phone was still pressed against his ear – pressed so hard that it was moist with contact sweat. The adrenaline was well and truly flowing. Any second now he was expecting more info – any info.

'He's entered the mall,' came the voice from the silence. 'Where are you? We can't track your exact position inside the centre.'

'I'm by Costa Coffee in the centre of the mall.'

'Good. Stand by.'

This was it – this could be the end. He didn't have enough information. He felt useless. All he could do was look around and check for the usual signs. It was summer and hard to conceal an explosive vest under a t-shirt, so someone in big baggy clothing could be the target.

He looked over at Next, near where he was standing. Nothing unusual there – just single guys leaning by the windows waiting for their partners. And down towards Subway – but that was the wrong direction, unless the target had gone round to the south side before entering. There had been enough time. A couple of men from an ethnic minority approached him from that direction.

'Al, I need to know if the target definitely entered the mall from the north.'

'Yes, from the north.' That cleared the men on the south side. He looked towards Optical Express – the direction of the threat. It was clear, as far as he could see. Busy, but clear.

'Come on, come on, Al. I need something.'

'It's coming in now; he's nearly on top of you. Surveillance has ID'd the suspect. I'm hanging up now, emailing you the photo.' Cam held the phone in front of him and waited. He wiped the sweat that had collected on the screen of the phone and continued to wait. Only a few seconds had passed but it felt like an eternity.

'Jesus Christ, come on!' He looked up and down between the phone and the mall extending towards the optician's. Still nothing suspicious. It was then it dawned on him – the signal was weak inside the mall. Panic gripped him as he started moving side to side round the coffee shop in the hope to find a pocket of reception.

Still the phone was blank. He gave up and pocketed the phone in his top. There was nothing more to do but head into the danger area. He moved forward, looking at everyone – each individual face. He looked for signs of anxiety, beads of sweat or general nervousness – but with no success. He fished out the phone.

'Shit!' He had not felt the phone vibrate in the loose pocket of his hooded top. The email opened and he read the single line of text.

Take suspect alive!

'What?' The photo was taking its time to download. It appeared, but was pixelated, slowly coming into focus.

'Come on! Come on!' Then it was there. He stopped and stared at it in disbelief.

The face that looked back from the screen could have been anyone in the mall. It was a white guy – a westerner – even similar-looking to Cam. He looked up from the photo and saw him straight away. Walking towards him, Cam was right – he was wearing a fleece that could easily hide a device… only Cam would never have suspected this man.

Following behind by about fifteen metres were two men carrying familiar bags. It was two guys from the troop. Cam knew he was covered. One would be the operator who could disarm the device and the other would be carrying counter-measure equipment so it could not be set off remotely. 'All I have to do is take him down.'

The man had his hands in his pockets. That could be where the initiator switches are and his fingers are on the trigger. Cam turned to look in the window of John Lewis and let the man walk past. The suspect wasn't looking round – he was too focused on what he was about to do. And that was to kill himself and as many innocent civilians as possible and to cause as much fear as he could.

Once the man was directly behind him, he turned and bent down. Cam had never moved faster. He grabbed the man's ankles and pulled them from underneath him. The suspect jerked forward and pulled his hands from his pocket to stop his fall. It was a natural human instinct, and it happened automatically, taking his fingers away from the buttons in his pockets.

The man slammed to the floor and Cam was on top, pressing his face into the ground and breaking his nose. He straddled the man high up on his back and sat on his shoulder blades. He forced his knees under the man's armpits, rendering his arms useless.

The crowded mall watched on in shock and horror as Cam assaulted this man, apparently completely unprovoked. Cam knew it wouldn't be long before some have-a-go hero would be dragging him off the suspect. Thankfully the two guys from the troop were there within seconds. The suspect was zip-tied, feet and ankles, and the operator was straight in there with his tuff -cuts cutting off the fleece. His main focus was to make the device safe.

'Police! Don't move!' The warning rang out across the mall. 'Get back! Get back!' It was time for Cam to go. In moments he was off the man and into the crowd which was being herded back away from the scene. He didn't know if the police were aware of his presence or were too hyped up to notice, but he was able to blend into the multitude of people.

He pushed his way towards the exit, only to hear, 'You. you!'

Cam stopped and turned expecting to see an eagle-eyed police officer. What he saw was a man with a digital camera, snapping away. The spark of the flash was eclipsed among the others – only this one was pointing at him. Cam stepped in towards the photographer and snatched it out of the man's hands.

'Hey! What the fu…?'

'Shut up and back off!' Cam said before the man could finish.

Once he made it outside he smashed the camera to the floor, splintering it into pieces. He sifted through the wreckage and picked out the memory card. Once out of sight of the mall he ducked into an alley. He leant his back against the alley wall and caught his breath. He couldn't believe he had got out of there. Then the phone buzzed once again.

Task complete. Stand down.

He looked at the memory card in his hand and after fiddling it around his fingers he slipped it into his pocket. Might be a nice souvenir.

Chapter 21

It took a long time to get back to the flat – the city was locked down. It seemed every agency in the country was in Edinburgh. When he finally made it back he went straight to his television and turned it on.

The story was breaking all over Sky News and the presenters were doing their best to piece together what was actually going on in Scotland's capital city. 'WE HAVE REPORTS OF A MASSIVE TERRORIST PLOT IN EDINBURGH CITY CENTRE, DETAILS ARE SKETCHY. HOWEVER, THE INFORMATION COMING INTO THE STUDIO NOW SUGGESTS THE POLICE HAVE AVERTED THE PLOT AND HAVE A SUSPECT IN CUSTODY.'

Cam stood in the living room, close to the flat screen on the wall and watched as the scene changed to aerial views of the streets surrounding St James's Centre. Police officers directed the public away from the shopping centre as they cordoned off the entire city centre. The yellow news bar at the bottom of the screen showed the same breaking news over and over again. 'TERRORIST PLOT THWARTED BY POLICE. EDINBURGH

UNDER ATTACK- and -POSSIBLE SUICIDE BOMBER IN POLICE CUSTODY.'

As he watched he could scarcely believe that he was involved in all this. Less than an hour ago he was right there, and now he was safely back home. He realised that he had just been involved in most probably the biggest threat to national security in recent history. 'I think I deserve a drink.'

He poured himself a generous double whisky and sat back on the sofa to watch the story unfold. He wondered if the whole story would come out – or would the government keep some things back, as they normally did?

Just when he thought the day's events were over, the phone rang. He answered it, thinking that maybe his part in all this was not yet over.

'Hello.'

'Hello Cam, how does it feel to be a hero?'

'Absolutely terrifying. I was sure I wasn't going to get out of that one. What the hell happened Al? Why were you so slow with the updates? A second later and that would have been it.'

'I know. It got a little intense didn't it? But I promise you that you got it as we got it. You know how it is when different agencies try to communicate with each other. Especially when one of them doesn't officially exist.'

Cam didn't need to ask any more. He had plenty of experience with that sort of thing. Everybody wanted to be the one who saved the day, and sometimes they didn't disclose everything to the other departments – usually to the detriment of the operation.

'What's actually happening now? Is that it for me?'

'On this one yes, but sit tight. We are analysing the situation. This is a new one for us, we have been caught off guard and we need to figure out what to do next.'

'How do you mean a new one?'

'Well, it was a shock when his ID came through. We were just going to let you take him out, but when we realised he was a westerner we needed him alive.'

'What did he have on him?' asked Cam.

'I think it's best that you know only what you know already – or what you need to know. I'll give you all the information you need to complete your task, but that's it. OK?'

'Yeah, sure. I suppose.'

'Good. Now sit tight and I'll get back to you if we need you.'

'Alright – but Al, I was photographed by a passer-by while I was leaving the scene, but I got the camera off him. I'm not sure if anyone else noticed me. Am I going to be safe after this?'

'Don't worry about a thing; we will take care of all that from here. We have ways of making things disappear and you will remain anonymous. We will get you in and out and then cover your tracks afterwards, understand?'

'OK. Did you guys get me into the hub? I can't work out why the police officer just let me in.'

'Yes that was us; do as we say and it will all be sorted for you. Now are you happy with how it all went? Anything for me at this point?'

'Not off the top of my head – but perhaps some sort of Bluetooth device so I can talk to you without having to hold the phone up to my ear.'

'Good idea. I'll sort something out. Check your drop-location tomorrow. And if you think of anything else let me know.'

'OK, I will.'

'Good lad. For now, you are stood down. Well done for today. I'll be in touch.'

Cam put the phone down and sipped his whisky. Relaxing into his chair he turned his attention back to the screen. It was going to be interesting to watch from here, all the time knowing what had really gone on in St James' shopping centre.

* * * * * * *

As the days passed by, the hype began to die down; it was almost as if nothing had happened. For two days the public had been scared even to walk down the main street, terrified that the terrorists would strike again. But now, four days on and they had already forgotten. Things were nearly back to normal, only some small follow-up stories on the news. Cam was surprised that they had reported accurately with only a few things left out, such as his own involvement in the operation.

As Cam sat on the top of Arthur's Seat with the sun warming his face, he watched the people of Edinburgh go about their daily business. As the people passed him they had no idea that the lonely figure on the hillside was the man responsible for saving the city.

He would never receive any acknowledgement for his actions – but he wasn't the type to need that sort of attention. The police had seemed to be given most of the credit for this one; the troop had been conveniently left out again. They had been the ones who had made the device safe but nobody would ever know.

Cam thought back to the new members of the troop he had seen before the op started. He had never seen them before – but why would he have? The guys he served with were no longer around. It made him remember some of the times they spent together.

* * * * * * *

That day they had spent at an old abandoned American Air Force base in the summer of 2003 was one of their more relaxed training sessions, where Cam was allowed to blow up almost anything he wanted.

The exercise had been paused for lunch for about an hour and they were just finishing up the BBQ Swanny had cooked up. It was about time to get back to it – time for one more assault lane. This time round it was Cam's job to set up the trip wires, pressure mats and other devices for the team to make safe.

He had also been given a box of flash bangs to get rid of, and he was using them to simulate battle noises as distractions, trying to give the exercise more realism. For this practice, Cam had set up the usual devices for the team to deal with, but he had a surprise for them on this one.

He had wired together three flash bangs and hidden them in an electrical cupboard, and when the practice started he had positioned himself down the corridor with the initiator. From there he would wait until the team was near the cupboard, then set it off.

Cam held the claymore clicker and waited. He kept a check of where the team was by leaning out of the doorway he was in and peering down the corridor. The black figures sneaked along towards his position, checking everything they passed, as anything could be a hidden device.

As the team drew up to the electrical cupboard he ducked back inside the doorway and double clicked the claymore clicker. Click, click, BOOM!!! Cam looked in horror as the dirty white cloud of dust and shrapnel flew past the door down the corridor. He could feel the blast wave pass.

Once it quietened down he looked towards the electrical cupboard, to where the team should be. He remembered thinking that it might not have been the best idea to set it up like that. To have placed the flash bangs in the metal electrical cupboard, effectively made a pipe bomb.

As the dust cleared he could see some movement and hear coughing. He hoped he had not injured anyone, and he was worried he had until he heard the giggling from the coughing figures in the distance. Luckily they all shared the same sense of humour – the type most squaddies have.

Once the exercise was finished and it was time to get packed away and return to base, Cam had been instructed to use up the remaining flash bangs. It was always easier to use munitions up than deal with the paperwork of returning them. So off he went with Glenn to find more stuff to blow up.

Eventually they came across a toilet block and wondered what the flash bangs would do to the toilet cisterns.

'Do you think four together would do to it?' Glenn said.

'I think it'll blow the shit out of it.'

'Should we?' Glenn asked.

'I can't think of any reason not to – in fact I think we have to.'

'Yeah – in the interests of experimentation.'

'Yes, this is nothing more than a scientific experiment,' Cam said, as he dropped the linked-up flash bangs into the cistern and closed the porcelain lid over the top.

BOOM! This time he could feel it in his ears as the pressure wave blasted past where they had taken cover. When they looked there wasn't much left of the toilet – or even the cubicle it was in.

'What the hell was that?' the boss shouted, as he rounded the corner.

'We're – um – using up the flash bangs,' Glenn said.

'By blowing up the bloody toilets!' The boss seemed a bit upset and the two braced themselves for a bit of a telling off as they stood in front of the boss like naughty school boys.

The boss looked at the two culprits and sighed as he thought what to do with them.

'How many you got left?'

'Six, Sir,' Cam replied.

After a short pause a small smile appeared on the boss's face. 'Well let's see what six will do.'

By the time they had wired the last of the flash bangs together, the other members of the troop had turned up to witness the last of the explosions. Eight professional soldiers hiding behind a wall, giggling about blowing up a toilet.

BOOM! With ringing ears the guys slowly poked their heads up over the wall to see no toilet – just wreckage. Then in unison they looked up to see no roof – it had been blown right off. Only a hole remained, with dirty black smoke rising skyward.

'Someone's gonna see that shit!' Spike laughed.

'We better get the hell out of here,' the boss said, as he joined in the sniggering. The laughter continued most of the way home.

* * * * * * *

Cam sat on the hillside with a smile on his face. He could still hear the giggling and funny comments as he looked out over the city. But the laughter in his head faded as other memories took over.

The merriment turned to fear and the laughter to screams as the confused shouts for help echoed in the distance. He could hear the dazed and muffled screams, and as always the last thing he thought he heard was, 'Cam, where are you?' But it had faded. Then the phone rang, as if to say 'wake up!' It was Al.

'Cam, you're needed again. It's going to be a long one. You ready?'

'Um, can't speak at the moment,' he replied, as he cleared the unpleasant thoughts from his mind. 'Give me twenty minutes; I'll be home by then.'

Chapter 22

'I'm sending someone round. You're going to need help on this one.' Al's voice was as cool and well-spoken as usual.

'Who's coming? How will I know it's them?'

'You'll know,' was Al's reply. 'Listen to him; he will give you the brief on what needs to be done. From now on consider yourself active. You have free actions, and if you need anything let me know.'

'It's not the same guy as last time is it? Do you know the hassle he caused me?'

'Yes, I heard about that. Don't worry that was just George being George. He's a bit of a joker.'

'So it is him, then.'

'Yes it is; he'll be with you shortly.'

Cam didn't have to wait long until there was a knock at the door. He had been watching through his CCTV for someone to approach and enter the building. He hadn't seen anyone until the three knocks on the door. He did however recognise him immediately. It was the same man who had visited him just before the St James job.

'Hey Cam, how you doing?' He said as if they were best friends.

'Not too bad. Come in George.'

'I heard about what happened, good work,' said George as he sat down on the same stool as last time.

'I think there was a lot of luck involved,' Cam said, being modest. 'Coffee?'

Cam handed a cup of coffee to the man and joined him at the breakfast bar which separated the kitchen from the living area.

'Al said you have something for me?'

'Yeah. What do you know about Al-Qaeda's white army of terror?'

'Well, it's a relatively new thing. Over the past few years British non-Muslims are being recruited by Al-Qaeda. They are seen as perfect weapons as they blend in with the local population and won't raise any flags.'

'Do you know how many there are?' George asked.

'I've been out of the loop for a while now, but by my best guess, a good few hundred.'

'There's about one thousand five hundred that we know about. But there may be as many as two thousand. We just don't know. Not all of them will go down the path of becoming radicalised, but maybe two thirds will – and that is a significant number.'

'Most Islamic groups say that it is impossible to convert a westerner as we have very liberal lifestyles that aren't compatible with their religion. Praying five times a day, not drinking and a strict diet are all things they must do, that we would find hard to keep up. So they say it isn't happening, but we know it is.'

'So I take it this guy I got in St James is one of them,' Cam said.

'Yeah, but we'll get back to that. What do you know about their recruiting methods?' George asked.

'The weak-minded, the lonely, prisoners…'

'Good, tell me more about that,' George interrupted.

'Members of terror groups already serving in prison can spot potential new recruits – the young first-timers who are scared and in need of protection are easy prey. They take their time but over the weeks and months support and comfort will turn to religion. But how much of a threat are they?' Cam asked.

'New recruits into a religion are always a bit more fanatical than the ones who have grown up in it. They feel they have more to prove and that they must defend their new faith. They are extra sensitive to the apparent discrimination that we hold against them. We can't find them, we can't monitor them – they're a massive threat.'

'I only know of one – Richard Reid, the shoe bomber,' Cam interrupted. 'He was a joke; he can't be classed as a national threat. And I was part of the team who put his mentor away.'

'That was a few years back Cam – they are much more organised now. They are completely compartmentalised; they keep themselves to themselves and don't report to anyone. And we don't get any reports from the public about westerners – only on the ethnic population. We were having trouble locating them. That was until a few days ago.'

'So my guy is one of them?'

'It seems that way. The police who were watching them kept lots of important information back in the hope of being the ones who made the arrest, but it got way out of control, and it resulted in the St James job.'

'Did they get anything out of my suspect?'

'Not much, but we do have a little to go on. Come on let's go for a drive.'

* * * * * * *

Leaving the city and heading east, the two sat quietly. Cam was still unsure of where they were going. As George drove, Cam used his peripheral vision to look over at his driver. George was older then Cam – not by much, but maybe by a few years. He looked rough and unshaven – but still sharp. He was obviously an intelligent man and Cam could tell he was ex-military. He might look scruffy in his jeans and t-shirt, but soldiers couldn't get rid of that look they tended to have.

Cam was getting anxious; they had been driving now for over three-quarters of an hour. With Edinburgh well and truly behind them they made their way along the A1 towards Dunbar. The coast came into view and they kept going, passing the smaller villages that lay alongside the motorway.

The silence was starting to get to Cam; he normally didn't mind the peace and quiet but he had so many questions.

'So, where are we going?' He had to ask.

'Just here,' George replied, as he pulled into a lay-by.

'This is where we were going! What the hell's out here?'

'That,' George said, as he pointed into the distance.

'Torness Power Station. Are you going to tell me what's going on?'

George turned the engine off, undid his seat belt and shuffled round in his seat so he faced slightly more towards Cam.

'The man you stopped in the shopping centre was David Brant. He's thirty-two years old, a petty criminal and substance abuser. Born and bred in Edinburgh, he's never left the area and is a bit of a sad character. He's got nothing going for him and has no close friends, probably because of the drug use. In and out of prison his entire life; he was just paroled about five weeks ago. A real loser.'

George picked up his take-away coffee, which was now stone cold, and took a sip.

'Sounds it,' Cam said. 'So why did you bring me out here to talk about this idiot?'

'Because he works there.' George pointed towards the power station with his coffee cup.

Cam and George both turned towards the large nuclear station on the horizon.

'You're telling me a suicide bomber who tried to blow himself up in Edinburgh city centre works there, in a nuclear power station?' he said, still looking at the station.

'Yeah. He started there almost immediately after leaving prison. Just a low-level worker – nothing special. We've been interrogating him and he's just a sad loner who has no life outside prison. Now he has nothing except his job in there.'

'You get anything else out of him?' Cam asked.

'Very little,' George said, as he leaned forward and rested his forearms on the steering wheel. 'He is, however, a fanatic. He wasn't before prison, so we can only gather he was brainwashed while doing his time.'

'We're going to need more than that.' Cam said as he joined George by leaning forward on the passenger-side dashboard.

'There is more. Brant was released early,' George continued. 'Only on the condition of gaining employment. And the only reason he got out early was because he was given a job by one of the upper-level managers in there.'

'That guy sounds like a good place to start; do we know who he is?'

'Yes we do. Mr Richard Bell. You will get all the information that we have via email tonight.' George started the engine and fastened his seat belt. 'There's more. Bell has two more ex-cons working for him. Two guys with very similar stories to Brant.

Again, you will get their details tonight.' George pulled out of the lay-by and u-turned back towards Edinburgh.

'We're going to work together on this one, but you're to take the lead, so if you need any support, get in touch with Al and it will be arranged. Any further information or equipment is yours – again, arrange through Al.' Cam listened as they approached the outskirts of the city. 'This could be big. Find out who is involved, the makeup of their organisation and come up with a plan of how to take them out.'

They pulled up outside Cam's apartment block. He opened the car door and stepped out. As he closed the door, George lowered the electric window. He leaned over on to the passenger side and looked up at Cam. 'Wait for those emails and get to work. Keep Al updated. See you soon.'

* * * * * * *

People outside the window were walking down the street as if nothing was going on – but in their world, nothing was. Cam sipped his whisky as he waited for the emails to arrive. The computer was on and his email inbox was displayed on the screen. His head was full of questions, but he was certain he had to start with Richard Bell – the man who had secured the release of the prisoners.

The computer bleeped as the emails arrived. Four separate emails came in almost simultaneously. The emails were named 'Richard Bell', 'Steve Palmer', 'Phil Reilly' and 'Task Information'. Cam read all the emails carefully and printed out the profiles of the three men.

Bell was one of the managers of the station; he had got himself involved in some kind of jobs for ex-prisoners scheme. He noted his address and decided to pay him a visit later in the evening.

Palmer and Reilly had very similar profiles and histories to David Brant, the St James bomber. They both had long criminal records – mostly petty crimes and drug addiction.

The fourth email was a hard copy of everything George had told him. It was obvious that Bell had a plan for the two ex-criminals. A similar fate was in their future. Cam knew they didn't have much time – with the failure of the St James job, Bell would be sure they would be on to him. He would most probably bring his plan forward.

Cam had a few questions for Al, but they could wait until after he checked out Bell's house. Maybe then he would have more of an idea of what he would need to complete this task. The light was fading; it was time to head to the more affluent area of Edinburgh.

Cam unplugged his phone from the wall; he wanted it to have a full battery for the night. He also pocketed the small Bluetooth headset Al had sent him after he requested it. His silenced P226 and his lock-pick set completed the equipment he might need that night.

Cam got into his car and pulled out of the underground car park. He realised he had had a couple of whiskies earlier – but he was in complete control; it would take more than a few drams to influence him, although he was definitely over the legal limit. He wondered how far Al's authority stretched.

Where Bell lived was well-maintained and lit by street and lawn-lights. Large houses with huge double garages lined the long, straight road. The street was wide and flanked by expensive cars parked up outside the mansions. Bell had done all right for himself, thought Cam. He parked up and began what could be a long night. Luckily the day had been very warm; the heat had been absorbed into the tarmac and bricks and was now keeping the night air at a pleasant temperature.

Cam studied the information on Bell, and noted the type of car he had. Cam looked up and down the street and realised that nearly everyone on the street had that type of car. Obviously a 'must-have' around there. Every time a car drove past it could have been him.

Bell finally arrived back home just after one in the morning. As he pulled up and waited for the automatic garage door to open, Cam wondered where he had been until this early hour. He might have been at work – or could he have been somewhere else? He wanted to know what he had been up to but there was no way of finding out.

Cam watched as he drove into the garage and the door came down. After a short time the lights in the garage went off. Cam could see the route Bell took as he moved through the house, by following the trail of lights as they were turned on then off. He finally spent some time in what could be the kitchen before moving upstairs. After an hour, all the lights went off.

Cam saw nothing suspicious in Bell's actions. He could have been anyone at all – just coming home, perhaps having a cup of tea and then going to bed. Should he enter the house and snoop around? Too risky. If Bell was not spooked by the failure of the St James job, then there was no point in making him paranoid.

Cam decided to return home, but on the way back to his apartment he took the long way and went past the homes of both Palmer and Reilly. Only Reilly was still up, with lights on at the back of the house. The contrast in the two homes was huge. Reilly's house was only about the size of Bell's garage.

Cam got out of his car and, after making sure it was locked, walked round the side of Reilly's house and jumped the rusty metal railings. He peered through a side window that looked into a hallway at the bottom of the stairs. He jumped back in shock as he almost came face to face with a man sitting on the stairs. The man was hunched over as if in pain, but Cam could not see what he was doing. As the lights were on in the hallway, the man would not be able to see Cam looking in. Cam could watch as long as he wanted.

The man straightened up and nearly lay back on the staircase. Cam now knew what he was doing. It was Reilly and he was still using. Reilly released the tourniquet on his forearm and let it drop to the floor. He sighed and closed his eyes and lapsed into unconsciousness. Cam wondered what the hell could be so good about that – and he also wondered if Bell knew about it. Devout Muslims were supposed to stay clear of all that. 'This might work to my advantage,' Cam thought.

He got back in his car and began composing an email to Al. He requested that Al find out all three men's work schedules. They all worked a shift pattern and he wanted to know when they would be out of their houses. Also he asked to know more about the two criminals and their time in prison. He then drove home.

By the time he was back in his apartment Al had replied to his email. Cam poured himself another double and sat in front of the computer. The email contained some interesting information.

Cam, we have been looking into the three targets' shift patterns. All three are working the late shift tomorrow night. They're all on 'til two in the morning. The station will be at its lowest manning; perhaps you might like to exploit it. Bell's office is in the main building; his window overlooks the perimeter fence on the west side. I've provided a station schematic in the attachment to this email. We are still looking into the prisons files on your other matter. Formulate a plan and keep me updated.

Cam opened up the attachment and printed a hard copy. He sat for a short while and sipped his drink. He studied the plans of the station, paying particular attention to Bell's office. When he had come up with a plan, he emailed Al to let him in on what would happen the next night. He also asked for some equipment to be delivered: a standard army-issue day sack, a laser microphone with a record function and a ghillie suit. Cam wanted to remain as undetectable as possible outside the wire of the station. He had used Google Earth to get a good view of the surrounding terrain; the ground was a dry mixture of sand and long, light grass with sporadic gorse bushes. With that in mind Cam asked for a ghillie suit of a light colouring.

Al's reply was short and sweet.

> *Approved. I would like George to accompany you on this one. He will be equipped as you will be. Expect him early evening.*

'Fair enough,' thought Cam. The more the merrier. But for now it was time for bed – the next night would be even longer.

Chapter 23

Cam woke early, anticipating the day ahead. He knew, however, that he would need more sleep. He turned over and closed his eyes. George was not due until the afternoon – plenty of time to sleep. The odds were that they would be up most of the night.

When he finally got up it was gone midday. After a bite to eat he took a trip down to the car park. As Cam raised the boot of his car he saw a standard army day sack sitting in the middle of his boot. He swung it over his shoulder and closed the car and turned the key to lock it.

When he got back into his apartment he rolled up the carpet that covered a small portion of the wooden living-area floor. 'This might get a bit messy,' Cam thought. He pulled the contents from the day sack and placed them on the floor. He opened the green padded pouch that contained the laser mic. The kit consisted of a combined laser mic and a receiver which had a built-in amplifier and recording system. There was also a small extendable tripod that would hold the laser steady. Cam was impressed – a system like that could cost up to ten thousand pounds. The laser would be used to record any conversations that would take place in Bell's office. As the occupants of the room talked to each other, the sound waves from the voices would cause the windows to vibrate ever so slightly. The laser would bounce off the glass and back to the receiver, allowing the operator to listen to and record any conversations taking place in the room, without ever going near the office.

Next came the messy bit. He unrolled the ghillie suit on the floor. He would have preferred to have made his own, but time constraints forced him to use a manufactured suit. This, however, was well-constructed, made from lengths of hessian sack, soaked in slightly differing colours of mud. These strips of hessian were attached to the back of a pilot's flight suit; an extra attachment connected to the rear of the neck could be pulled up and used as a hood. It even smelt earthy; Cam thought that it had definitely been made by a professional sniper. The shades of the strips were about right for the terrain he would be covering. Any customisation could be done with grass, twigs or any of the local foliage once on location.

He placed the laser mic kit at the bottom of the day sack, then rolled up the ghillie suit, which he packed in the day sack on top of the mic. In the side pouch he placed his silenced pistol, already in its holster and belt. Along with the pistol he put in some extra magazines filled with 9mm ammo. In the other side pouch he put a filled, two-litre water bottle and some Snickers bars. The top flap had some warm kit in it – gloves, hat and a shamagh – standard stuff.

With the day sack ready by the front door there was nothing left to do but wait for George to arrive and the light to fade. It was after eight at night when George knocked on the door. Inside they sat at the breakfast bar and Cam prepared a cup of tea. Tea was part of the process; tea was usually drunk by British troops before a mission or a battle. Even American troops had slowly started to appreciate tea as opposed to coffee, and had started to drink it too... although they would never admit it.

'So, Al gave me a brief about tonight, how do you want to handle it?' George said.

'Well, we're going to put our kit into one of our cars; Al's given you the kit list, right?'

'Sure, it's in my car; we'll take mine shall we?'

'Yeah. OK, then we'll head out to Torness and pull up in one of the parking places a few miles from the station. Make our way on foot to the west side of the plant, hide up, laser Bell's office window and wait. Hopefully we'll hear something useful. Bell and the others are on 'til two in the morning. Maybe with them all together and the plant being quiet they might talk more freely.'

'Cool. Happy with that. Are we expecting any trouble?'

'No, not a thing. The Civil Nuclear Constabulary don't patrol outside the wire, so apart from some random act of God, I'm not expecting any difficulties.'

'Good.' George finished his tea with one final gulp.

'Let's get going then.'

The night was clear and a bit colder than the previous ones. With no cloud cover there was nothing to keep the warmth in. The stars were starting to appear as they drove out of the city and the artificial light faded into the distance. It was going to be a bright night, as the full moon was flooding the open area with silver light. Cam saw a sign for a parking area half a mile ahead.

'I think this is close enough. Shall we pull up here?'

'Yes mate, should take us about an hour to walk the rest.'

As the two men got out of the car, Cam had a look up and down the road for signs of headlights. With no sign of any approaching cars, George opened the boot and handed Cam his day sack. George grabbed his backpack – a green Berghaus thirty-litre. George obviously liked to buy his own equipment, but Cam never had a problem with issue kit and found it good enough for what he needed.

With the bags on their backs, George pulled up the false floor of the boot to reveal a HKSL8 semi-automatic rifle with an attached night sight.

'Christ! Do you know something I don't?' Cam exclaimed.

'You have to be prepared,' George said looking at Cam, almost disappointed that he wasn't tooled up.

'Come on – we better get a move on.'

Before they moved off the road into the countryside, George opened the driver's door and pulled something from the glove-box. He locked his car then attached the sign to the front windscreen. It read 'Police Aware'.

'Nice one,' Cam said. He was impressed; he liked it when people thought of the small details. He would remember that little trick.

'Like I said, you have to be prepared.' George now wore a slight smile and looked a little bit smug. 'Come on, let's go.'

* * * * * * *

The ground was open and brightly lit by the moon – not the best for moving about undetected. Luckily they were not expecting any surprises. The two men kept at least ten metres apart and moved slowly and carefully, all the time looking all around three hundred and sixty degrees for any unusual movement apart from their own.

After getting a good distance away from the road they stopped. Both knelt down and dragged their ghillie suits from the bags. They put them on and closed the fronts. Ties had replaced the zips, which could get jammed if you were going to be crawling around on your belly. Cam then put on the leg holster and wrapped the thigh-strap securely round his leg. He got George to pull the hessian strips out from under the belt to conceal the weapon, and they did the same when the day sacks were back on.

Once the two men resembled walking bushes, they moved off towards the power station in the distance. George put his rifle into his shoulder and walked forward as silently as he could. Cam watched and thought he had better draw his pistol and patrol with it in his hands. He knew they didn't need to, but George seemed to want it.

It must have been about eleven as they approached the station. They were a few hundred metres away from the perimeter fence and they needed to find a hide. There were plenty of gorse bushes around, but they needed to find the best one – one that would conceal them and their equipment, and also offer a good view of the window that was now in sight. Cam knew that was the window because he had studied the plans earlier in the day – also it was one of the few with a light on. So Bell was in his office, and they needed to get a move on and start recording.

They chose the bush they were going to use. They removed their day sacks and put them down in front of them and started to crawl forward. The best way to conceal yourself was to crawl through not back into; that way the bush would cover you and wouldn't be disturbed in the direction of the target.

Once in the bush, Cam started to set up the laser mic and tripod. With the tripod stuck into the ground to hold the mic steady, Cam began to aim it through the sight. All the time George was watching the fence and buildings for the Civil Nuclear Constabulary.

'Hope this works,' Cam said. There was still the possibility that it wouldn't. If the glass was rippled or frosted like in a toilet or even multi-laminated glass, it would not reflect the laser properly.

'OK, got it,' Cam said. He let go of the mic carefully, so as not to move it – even a millimetre would knock it off-line. Cam gently pressed the record button and waited. With the earpiece in, he should hear everything.

'Do you hear anything?' George asked.

'I think I hear movement – little movements, like typing. Someone is definitely in there.'

As the time passed they started to doubt their plan. They had been in the hide for over an hour now, and still only recorded typing, coughing and chair scrapes. They had heard nothing useful. Cam started to think maybe he should have checked out their houses instead. He hoped he hadn't made a bad decision.

'Got movement – inside the wire, CNC patrol,' George said calmly.

'OK, shouldn't be a problem.' Cam was happy they were well-concealed. Even the moon was behind them, so there would be no reflections off the night scope or laser mic lens.

'It's a dog section.' George was still calm, even though he must have been thinking like Cam. There was only a slight wind, but it was behind them and the wind would take their scent right towards the guard dog.

'Christ,' Cam said.

'Wait, wait.' George was watching as the two nuclear police with their dogs made their way along the fence line… all the time waiting for the dogs to start signing some sort of a presence. However, luck was on their side, and the patrol moved on, missing them completely. George didn't even remove the scope from his eyes; Cam looked over at him and admired the professionalism.

Cam wondered what had George done before getting involved with Al. He must have been Special Forces.

Cam's mind started to drift – back to his little ambulance station and the nice quiet life he had managed to carve out for himself. He wasn't meant to be doing this sort of thing; he wasn't in the military any more. But here he found himself. 'You are what you are,' he thought.

'Come in, sit down, the others should be here in a moment.'

'Got something!' Whispered Cam. George remained focused on his job as cover.

'Are they all coming to this meeting?'

'Yes, and I expect you to treat them as a valued part of this mission.' 'This must be Bell; this man has a commanding voice,' Cam thought.

'They're just so dumb.'

'I know, but they are vital to our cause. So just play the game.'

'Yeah, yeah OK.' There was then a silence for a few minutes.

'Steve, Phil, hello. How are you guys finding it here?'

'It's fine, I suppose,' answered a lone voice.

'Sit, sit.' 'That was Bell speaking,' Cam thought. He could now tell whose the voices were that were involved in the conversation.

'Do you guys fancy a drink?'

'No Sir, thank you,' came a nervous response.

'Steve, Phil, please don't be put off by what has happened over the past few days. Look, you knew Dave, but he was nothing to do with us, he must have been taking things into his own hands. He was acting alone and messed up big-time. Nothing to do with our plans – we are completely in the clear and ready to proceed with our mission. I do have your loyalty, don't I?'

'Yes Sir,' came a hesitant response.

'Good, I'll be in touch by the usual method. Get yourselves home and get some sleep. Off you go.'

After some chair scrapes and movement, Cam heard in his earpiece:

'For God's sake. I understand the use of these criminals, but can we trust them? Brant was a huge fuck-up – and these two aren't much better.' After a pause and a sigh, Bell continued.

'I know, but this is what we have to work with. We both know these guys are losers, but we have to make the best of what we've got. Let's do this thing – and then get out of here, OK?'

'Yeah, sure – just don't let it be another St James fiasco. OK?'

'It won't.'

'Good.'

And that seemed to be it. Nothing much more came out of Bell's office. Cam heard Bell finish up his daily duties and lock up his office before heading home. Cam had recorded all he could; it was time to go. He closed down the mike and replaced it in its pouch, folded up the mike stand and put all the bits and pieces into his backpack. The two men slowly crawled backwards out of the gorse bush, knelt up, looked at each other and made off towards their waiting ride home.

* * * * * * *

As George drove through the night towards the glowing light of Edinburgh, he and Cam discussed the night's events, and Cam removed the recording device from his day sack.

'I definitely got Bell and his two cronies, but the fourth voice – no idea.'

'Well, Al might be able to do something with the recording.'

'I hope so. I'll email it to him when I get back. I went to their houses last night, just to check them out.'

'Anything interesting?' George asked.

'Not much – didn't want to enter Bell's house, just in case. Reilly though, is still using drugs – saw him shooting up.'

'Great! A drugged-up suicide bomber. That's all we need.'

George pulled into the car park under Cam's building and the two men made their way up to the apartment.

Cam fired up the computer and began downloading the recorded conversation to his desktop, while George poured two glasses of Jack Daniels. He handed one to Cam as he was sending off the email to Al detailing the night's findings with the recording attached.

'Thanks,' Cam said as he took the glass and had a sip.

'What do you think Al's going to want us to do?'

'What makes you think I know?' George replied, as he drank back half his drink.

'Well, you've been with Al's lot longer than I have – you must have some idea.'

'Well,' George started as he poured himself another JD, 'if it's going to pan out like most of the other jobs, we're gonna have to take them out.'

'So we are pretty much just assassins?'

'Pretty much,' said George. 'But we take out the bad guys.' With that he downed his drink.

'Well, if we're going to kill them we should do it when they're all together. Like tonight,' Cam mused.

'Yeah, so we've got a week to put a plan together. Well, I'm off. I'll be in touch tomorrow, when Al's got back to us.'

'OK George mate, thanks for your help tonight.' George opened the door and stepped out into the corridor.

'I'll probably see you tomorrow. Good night, Cam.'

'See you later.' Cam closed the door.

After George left he topped up his drink. JD was a new thing for him – usually a scotch drinker, he decided to give it a try when he saw it on offer. He was almost ashamed to admit that it was good. It probably joined his favourite list along side Whyte and Mackay and Teachers. He never thought he would enjoy an American whisky.

He sat waiting for a reply from Al; he had no idea when it would come. There was no chance that he would be given any more tasks tonight, so it was safe to have a few more whiskies. Cam started to relax as he slowly sipped his JD. The sun would be up soon, he thought, as he looked towards his living room window. His eyes felt tired – he had been up for what felt like forever. Slumped on his sofa, he fell asleep with his glass resting on his stomach.

It was the light seeping through the blind that woke him. He squinted as he sat up and as he did so the glass fell and bounced across the floor.

'Shit!' He stood up and rubbed his face with his hands, trying to wake up. He glanced over at the computer screen; it indicated he had an email waiting. He stumbled over to the computer and sat down on the black swivel chair.

From the info you provided we have identified four individuals. The first three: Bell, Reilly and Palmer, you already have profiles of. The fourth is Doug Roberts, another high-level manager at the plant. Attached is his profile. He and Bell are the protagonists of this group and Palmer and Reilly are most probably being groomed for further attacks – most likely in the same vain as the St James one. They are communicating by disposable mobile phones that they renew every few days. This makes it very difficult to intercept. You are to eliminate all four. Make it quick, they are planning something. Use all means at your disposal, if you need anything, you know what to do. Good luck.

Cam printed the profile of Doug Roberts and added it to those of the other three. He flicked through the pages, absorbing every piece of information about these people. He wondered what they had planned. What did Bell have in mind for his two junkie puppets?

'Hey Cam, it's George.'

'Hi George.' Cam turned on the loud speaker of his mobile and held it close to his ear.

'What you get from Al?'

'We are to take them out – all four of them.'

'When?'

'Soon as possible. I suggest next week when they are all back on shift together.'

'That's what I thought. How we going to get in?'

'I thought, keep it simple and hop the fence.'

'I like simple. We need to know if the perimeter fence has PIDS.'

'I'll check it out tonight. I'll have a gander at their security systems and get back to you.'

'OK, good. Keep in touch.'

'Speak to you later.' With that he hung up. 'Looks like I'm back out tonight,' he thought. 'I need some sleep.'

Chapter 24

Once again, Cam found himself in the same gorse bush as the previous night. This time he was alone and the clear night had turned cloudy. That made the night darker and Cam felt more at ease. He was better concealed than the night before.

He watched and tried to time the guard patrols to see if they were regular. As it turned out they were not – they were random. The only thing he could be sure of was that after a patrol passed, he would have at least ten to fifteen minutes until another one went by – some with dogs, some without – also completely random.

He looked along the fence line; he pulled out his binoculars from his pocket and looked the full length of the perimeter. There were cameras, but they were few and far between. They looked like the kind of cameras that could be moved by remote control. However, Cam hadn't seen them move the whole time he had been there. Cameras could easily be tampered with but that would undoubtedly bring unwanted attention. He decided that it would be best to avoid them – that wouldn't be too hard; there were long stretches that weren't covered.

Next he needed to know if the fence that surrounded the station had PIDS. If it did, it could be a problem. Perimeter Intrusion Detection Systems could be installed into fences of all kinds. They registered movement on the fence and alerted guards to an exact point that was being tampered with. Cam would need to ascertain if it was in operation there.

Cam sat and watched, waiting for the next patrol to go by. He saw a two-man patrol come into view; they moved slowly along the inside of the fence line. They were observant and professional. The CNC were known to be a very good, well-trained police force. Cam watched them disappear into the distance, and he knew it was time to move.

He crawled forward out of the bush and into the open. It was just over a hundred metres to the fence line. Cam knelt up and slowly crept forward, staying vigilant all the time. Another patrol could appear at any time. He looked like a small bush in his ghillie suit as he approached the fence. He reached out his hand and rattled the fence. He then turned and ran back to the safety of the gorse bush.

Once back in the bush and completely concealed, he waited again. It wasn't long before a patrol vectored in on the exact area that he had rattled. Their flash-lights checked the fence for damage or tampering. They would obviously not find anything and when they didn't they said something into their radios and moved off.

'So, they definitely have PIDS,' Cam thought. He knew they would have to get round the problem. Luckily he had done it before and knew how to proceed. It was a time-consuming process, but they had five more nights before they moved in on the targets.

Cam walked back to his car. It was parked in the same place he and George had used the night before. He arrived at the car and opened the door and removed his newly acquired 'Police Aware' sign from his windscreen. He'd call George tomorrow; they needed to get started on the PIDS issue.

* * * * * * *

'George, good morning.'

'Hey Cam, how's it going?'

'Good mate. I went back to Torness last night and checked out their security.'

'What you get?'

'Well, surveillance cameras won't be a problem, looks like they are under-funded and need to update their CCTV system. But they do have PIDS.' Cam paused.

'Did you get any info on their patrol patterns?' asked George.

'That's another thing; they are good on their patrols. No patterns, completely random. You have at least ten minutes once one passes. They were right on when I aggravated the PIDS – not much time to play with.'

'Do you have a plan?'

'Yes I do,' Cam replied. 'I've done this before.'

'OK, I'm listening.'

'Right, here's how we're gonna handle this,' Cam began. 'We're going to take it in turns to aggravate their PIDS. Every night at about midnight, one of us will rattle the fence. The section directly opposite our gorse bush. I'll do Saturday and Monday, you do tonight, Sunday and Tuesday. Remember, midnight.'

'Yeah sure, I think I know what you're up to.'

'Good, so you'll go tonight?'

'No probs bud.'

'Good. Also prep for an infiltration op for Wednesday.'

'Yeah, I'm on it.'

'Good, I'll be in touch.'

With the conversation over, Cam had time to sit back, relax and think things over. He was going to have an easy night; George was going to Torness, so he might check out Doug Roberts' place. He didn't expect much – but it might be worth a look.

That night was dark, the weather was definitely turning. Cam found himself once again sitting in his car, watching a house he had never seen before. That was how all those things went. Nothing for hours and hours, followed perhaps by a short period of excitement. It required a specific type of person; not everyone could handle that type of work, remaining inconspicuous for long periods of time while remaining constantly alert.

Doug Roberts had been home most of the day; he only left for an hour and a half. As Roberts' car was hidden completely from view, Cam had managed to have a good look inside it. He was looking for items of interest that he might have left lying around. As it happened, very little was left on display. He had, however, noticed the mileage on the dashboard. When Doug returned he once again checked the mileage – he had travelled thirty-eight miles. Cam spent some time measuring distances on his street map. Doug might have visited either Bell or Reilly. It was impossible to tell who he'd visited; it might have been neither of them, completely unconnected.

He looked up from his street map, Roberts was clearly visible talking on a mobile phone. He was shouting into it, obviously very angry. He was really giving it some. Cam noticed the phone was a colourful-looking cheap one. He realised a man like Roberts wouldn't have a phone like that, he would have an expensive smart phone. Obviously one of those disposable things Al was on about. Cam almost got out of his car – he even had his hand on the door handle. He fidgeted in his seat but resisted the urge to get out – he had to be careful. It wasn't worth blowing it on this. Instead he sat back and watched as Doug finished his call and threw the phone across the room. 'What the hell was that about?' he thought, as he looked at his watch. It was half eleven at night. 'I wonder if George is where he should be.'

As it happened, he was. George was kneeling behind the gorse bush, looking through his night scope. He was waiting for his moment. Cam had been right, it was very hard to judge the right moment; the patrols were random and plentiful. He checked his watch – eleven thirty-five. He had to go for it; time was slipping away.

The two figures rounded the corner, just out of view. It was now or never. George was up and sprinting for the fence – it was not ideal, but he needed to get it done. He reached the fence, gripped it with his fingers and gave it a good shake. The fence twanged as it sprang back into place. George turned and ran – he felt like he was a child again back in Ireland, running from the doorbell he had just rung.

He had only just managed to get back to the bush as a four-man patrol along with a barking dog arrived at the spot of the shaken fence. George lay prone on the ground, the damp, coarse grass slowly soaking into his trousers. Lights flashed erratically back and forth as the Nuclear Police Officers checked the fence. They inevitably found nothing wrong with the fence and eventually went back to their regular patrols.

With his work completed, George sneaked away from the power station and back to his car. He could feel the dampness of his trousers rubbing his legs as he hurried back across the scrubland. It was going to be an uncomfortable drive home.

In the meantime, Cam was checking something out. Doug was clearly unhappy. He could have visited either Bell or Reilly – so what was he upset about? Cam had a theory. He thought that Doug had visited Reilly and found him in a drug-induced state, just as he had, some nights previously.

* * * * * * *

Reilly's house hadn't changed – if anything it looked more run-down than last time. He jumped over the rusty railings again and crouched down under the window through which he had seen him before. A car went past on the road where Cam had left his own car. Nothing to do with either him or Reilly, but he waited until the road was quiet again.

The light in the hallway was off this time, so if he were to look in he would be visible from inside the house. He raised his head and peered in the bottom left corner of the window – the stairs were clear. He now looked round into the doorway that led to another room – clear.

He moved round to the back yard. More rubbish littered the paved garden; Cam was not surprised. Looking up he could see a light on in one of the upstairs rooms. Cam wanted to get a look. A drainpipe ran down the wall near to the window in question. He checked it out; it was secured to the wall and firmly connected to the guttering along the roof. Cam gripped the black-painted pipe and leaned back; he placed his feet flat against the pebble-dashed wall and began to climb toward the lit window. He moved foot over foot, hand over hand, until he was level with the windowsill.

Cam knew he could not be seen when he looked into the bedroom. Inside he could see no one. He climbed a little bit higher. He then saw the top of someone's head; someone was sitting at the foot of the bed. A few inches higher and he realised it was Reilly – spaced out again. He was slumped on the floor at the end of his bed. Cam climbed back down and stood in Reilly's yard.

He had to think about this. Had Doug come round, found Reilly doped up, left and gone home and phoned Bell? Could that be why he was so pissed off? Was one of his bombers hooked on drugs, and putting their plans in jeopardy? If Doug had been there and Reilly was in that state, the door would probably be unlocked as he wouldn't be able to lock it from the outside. Cam walked round to the front and tried the front door. It opened.

Chapter 25

'How'd it go last night?'

'Good, shook the fence at about half eleven, guards checked it out and left after about five minutes.'

'Good,' Cam said. 'I checked out Roberts' house. I think he went round to Reilly's and found him out of his head. He then called Bell and had a heated conversation. I could be wrong though, but I'm worried they might bring their next op forward.'

'Maybe,' replied George. 'But we have to stick to the plan; it's all resting on you getting in there on Wednesday night.'

'Yeah, I know. Well I'm going tonight; I'll let you know how it goes.'

'All right, later.'

Cam sat and tried to compile a list of equipment that he might need for Wednesday. He would have to gain entry to the plant undetected, get into the building and find Bell's office and kill the members of the cell – all four of them. Once he had thought of every eventuality, he emailed it off to Al. He received a reply almost instantaneously saying to expect it tomorrow in the usual place.

He spent the remainder of that day resting, but he also went for a run. It felt like he had been involved in this for months. In actual fact it had not even been two weeks. Still, it felt good to blast out a run, even if the weather was a bit miserable. He tried to get some sleep but found it hard – his mind was full of so many thoughts whizzing round his head.

That night he copied George. He rattled the fence, attracting the attention of the guards. Not much had changed. Cam hoped his plan would work, but the signs were not encouraging.

All that changed two nights later when it was Cam's turn again. It was the Monday before the planned attack. Cam had returned to the gorse bush, a little worried they might be leaving too much of a trail. The grass had started to get flattened over the five previous nights. Feeling a little nervous that someone may have noticed, he made his move.

He dashed for the fence, gave it a rattle and hid himself back in the bush. This time, however, nothing happened. Had his plan worked? He waited, still nothing. 'It's worked; they've turned off the PIDS to that section of the fence.' Cam knew they would get sick of going to the same section night after night. They either thought it was malfunctioning or that it was some kind of animal movement. 'As long as it stays off,' he thought.

The next night George had the same result, and he relayed the information to Cam on the Wednesday morning.

'It's still off,' George said.

'Good, I'm going to contact Al; I'll get back to you.'

'Speak to you later.' Cam hung up. Tonight was the night. He was hit by a wave of nerves – these were dangerous and committed people, and it would not be easy.

He sent his final plan to Al, and he received the reply with the approval he needed, along with the usual wishes of good luck. He checked the equipment sent to him. Black clothing and Adidas assault boots – they were soft and silent. All the other items he ordered were packed into the black rucksack and tested for noise. He put on his equipment and jumped up and down; it sounded good.

'George, it's been approved.'

'So we're on for tonight?'

'Yes, we're good to go.'

* * * * * * *

Cam was waiting in the underground car park, ready to go. George would be there any minute. The light was fading and it was time to get going. George pulled up, Cam put his rucksack in the boot and got in. Nothing was said on the way to the drop-off point; they both knew the plan and the risks involved. That was enough to keep them both quiet.

They decided to approach from a different direction; they had overlooked one of the first rules of anti-surveillance: never set patterns. And they had. Over the last week they had used the same approach and egress route – even the same bush to hide in. The bush had started to show signs of damage. All it would take would be a suspicious guard to have a quick look outside the wire.

They drove past the road that led to the main gate. This was the most heavily guarded area of the plant, and he could never get in that way. They had to head to the section of fence they had worked on – that was his safe way in. George slowed to a stop on the main road, at a distance where the guards on the main gate would not be able to tell if the car was moving or not.

'I'll wait for your call, good luck,' said George. Cam looked at him.

'Thanks. Won't be long,' he said with a hint of sarcasm.

He moved quickly round to the corner of the car, but didn't get between the car's red rear lights and the front gate. He wanted to keep the illusion that the car was still moving. He reached over the boot and opened it, still keeping the rear lights on display. He retrieved his rucksack, quietly closed the boot then hid in the small ditch by the side of the road. Cam watched the car drive off, leaving him alone in the cool night breeze.

He swung his rucksack over his shoulders and pulled the shoulder straps tight. He pulled his balaclava from his pocket and pulled it over his head, slipped on his black sealskin gloves, connected his belt round his waist, the holster attached to his thigh with an elastic strap. On the elastic strap was his magazine-holder, and into this he slipped two full magazines.

Once ready, he started off. At a fast run he headed to the general area of the disarmed fence. It was a lot farther than the previous nights. It took nearly twenty minutes' run at a good speed to get there. Every so often he had to stop and lie flat on the ground to allow patrols to pass. As he approached, he identified another gorse bush to hide in. He crawled into it and pulled out his binoculars.

He watched a few patrols go past. He was waiting for a dog section; that way the next patrol would be at least ten minutes, and hopefully not a dog section. In preparation for the infiltration, he placed a set of rubber-handled wire cutters and a handful of zip ties in his pocket.

'Now, go.' He crawled out of the bush and ran for the wire. On arrival he skidded to a halt, looking to both sides for any movement that might make him retreat back to the safety of the hide. It was clear. He cut the wire with the cutters, from the ground up. Not too high, then off to one side – again not too far. The hole was just big enough to slide the rucksack through, then crawl after it.

He was in. He replaced the fence as best he could and secured it with the zip ties, trimming them to hide the fact the fence had been tampered with. Hopefully the next few patrols would not notice. He quickly surveyed his work. It looked good. With that he was off, running as fast as he could for the shadows of the nearest building as he swung his rucksack on to his back. He found a small shack near a doorway that would give him good cover; he got inside and waited in the shadows.

After fifteen minutes he got what he was waiting for. The next patrol was about to pass the cut fence. He watched as they closed in on the damaged wire. He held his breath as they walked right past. He sighed with relief, he would've liked to have had a dog unit pass to make sure his entrance was unnoticed, but he couldn't spare the time. He looked at his watch, hidden underneath an old cut-off green t-shirt sleeve. The sleeve was wrapped twice over his watch to hide the glowing face – an old trick from the jungle. He had to move immediately.

He had studied the schematics of the plant – he had spent hours memorising the doorways, corridors and outer areas that he would have to move through. He had also downloaded the maps to his phone, just in case he had to adapt his plan. After all, a plan never survived first contact. He had decided to enter through one of the outer buildings – one connected to the block that contained Bell's office.

Keeping close to the wall he ran, hunched over. He needed to make it to the edge of the building. He peeked round the corner and saw the unobservant patrol turning and disappearing into an alleyway. Once they were out of view, he followed. The door was just twenty or thirty metres away from his current position.

Cam skidded to a halt at his chosen entry point, and after a quick look at the door he reached for his lock-pick set. Al had supplied him with a professional set of picks, and with them he could pick this standard lock in seconds. When he felt the final pin of the lock settle into place, he slowly turned the handle. The door opened a few inches. The outbuilding was deserted and he slipped inside the cluttered, dirty room. As the door clicked shut he looked for a suitable hiding place – not a problem as the large room was strewn with debris.

Crouching under the wreckage of an old set of filing cabinets resting on a broken table, he waited and listened. It made sense to stop and wait after tampering with things such as fences and doors. He had to be sure he hadn't triggered any alarms or left any traces of his movement.

'Five minutes should be enough,' he thought. It was time to go. He stood up and took in his surroundings. The room was a large, open space, with a high ceiling, probably two storeys high. It was full of old office furniture, piled high. It was obviously a storage room for the offices in the next building. Cam walked around the tables and cupboards through the dusty warehouse to the eastern side of the room.

'Damn it!' Cam stood and looked at the combination lock that was keeping him out of the building he needed to get into. He looked desperately around the warehouse for an alternative entry point – maybe a vent. Then an idea occurred to him. He stooped down and took a handful of dust from the floor, turned and knelt down in front of the key-pad.

It was only a mechanical lock, not electric, so it shouldn't be alarmed. He held the dust in the palm of his outstretched hand took a deep breath and blew the dust on to the small metal keys. He then moved his face closer to the dust covered key-pad and blew again. The dust cleared from the lock – apart from five keys.

Luckily the last few people who had used the door had had greasy fingers to which the dust had stuck. The still dusty keys were C, 4, 2, 8 and 0. The way through the door would be to put these numbers in the correct order.

Cam tried various combinations of the numbers, pressing the C key in between tries. After the sixth attempt the door opened. As he inched it further open, the light from the other side streamed into the darkness of the storeroom. He was in. Now the real work began. He had to ascend four floors of the artificially-lit building, and then get into Bell's office, all the time avoiding anyone wandering the corridors. He hoped that they would be having another meeting like last week, they would then all be in the same room and easy to take out.

Chapter 26

Cam had the route burned into his mind, straight forward along the first corridor. Take a right and enter the stairwell. Up two floors, then out into the corridor again, almost double back towards the other end of the building and into the second stairwell. Up the final two floors, then Bell's office was on the west side of the block.

Cam could do nothing more than walk normally through the building. He would be listening carefully for movement, but if someone caught him by surprise he might be able to get away with it if he didn't act suspiciously. He removed his balaclava to try to appear that he belonged there. He knew it was a long shot, but there was nothing else he could do.

All was going well until he was half way up the first set of stairs. He stopped. Someone was coming. Whoever it was had just entered the stairwell, exactly where Cam had been just seconds previously. They were climbing the stairs towards him. Cam bounded up the stairs two or three at a time – anything to put some ground between himself and the person behind him.

He burst out into the corridor at the top of the flight of stairs; he had no time to look. He had his back to the wall as he looked back down the stairwell. The sound of someone climbing had gone; they must have only gone up one floor. Cam was never in any danger. He sighed with relief as he checked out the new corridor that he found himself in. He had to get to the other stairwell, all the way along the other side of the building. Then he heard another person coming towards him.

This time the person was walking down the corridor, in the direction he needed to go. He had to act fast – they were about to round the corner and literally bump into each other. In desperation he opened the nearest door and stepped inside. The room was dark and it took a few seconds for his eyes to adjust to the low light. His heart sank as he realised he had nowhere to go; he had chosen to hide in a stationery cupboard.

There was nothing more he could do but wait and hope that the person making the footsteps outside his useless hiding place wasn't after a stapler. As the person approached he drew his pistol from his holster strapped to his thigh. Then almost immediately replaced it. He couldn't kill an innocent person; if they found him he would just grab them, pull them into the cupboard, knock them out and wrap them up in scotch tape. After all, there was plenty of it on the shelves around him, he joked to himself.

His luck was holding out, the person walked right past. Another sigh and he cautiously opened the door and quickly made his way to the second stairwell. This time he made it to the top without any problems. This was it, he thought. He could see Bell's office. The door to his office was half frosted glass with his name in black print across it. He now saw Bell's title; he was a manager of something Cam had never heard of. He could see his light was on – Bell was in there.

Cam crept up to the door and looked through the corner of the frosted glass. He could see a figure sitting at a desk illuminated by a desk light. Bell must be catching up on some admin. Cam needed time to think, and he couldn't do that in plain view in the corridor. The next room along had a male toilet sign on the door. 'That will do,' he thought. Cam opened the door, bit by bit; it was dark inside until the automatic light came on. That meant nobody was in there, or the automatic light would have been on already. He made for one of the cubicles and locked it behind him.

He looked all around as he considered his next move. Above him the ceiling of the toilets was made of soft white mineral fibre squares. He stood on the toilet seat and moved one of the panels to one side. Standing on the cistern he looked into the darkness of the compartment above the toilet room. If he reached up he could grab some metal piping and pull himself up into the roof space. He pulled himself up with all his might, disappearing into the hatch he had created in the roof. Once clear of the roofing partitions, he swung his feet on to the area that was strengthened by the partitioning wall. Carefully balancing where he imagined the wall to be, he replaced the panelling to conceal himself in the crawl space above the ceilings.

He found himself in a very precarious situation. With the panel back in place he moved his attention to the other side of the wall he was resting on. He knew if he put his weight on any wrong section he would fall straight through it and go crashing to the floor. He wanted to get a look into Bell's office, but the only way to do that would be to prize up one of the roofing panels and look in that way. There was one panel that was much smaller than the rest; it was in the corner of the room and had been cut to size. That would be the one he would lift, and with it being smaller, it would be far less likely to break or make a noise as it was moved.

He also had to be aware that as it moved it would drop dust and scrapings on to the floor. But with it being in the corner of the office, and behind where Bell was sat, that would hopefully go unnoticed.

Cam inched his way along the top of the wall towards the small panel. Once he lifted it away he could lower his face to the hole in the roofing. He now saw Bell; he was still working away alone in his office. The room below was a well-decorated, good-sized office; it was furnished to a high standard. On the other side of the room was an en suite bathroom, with the door almost closed. That was the next place Cam needed to get to. From that room he could wait for everyone to gather – or at least take out Bell. If he could get rid of the leader, perhaps the cell would fall or disappear from the face of the earth.

Cam once again reached up for the pipes that ran the length of the building. Gripping with his hands, he raised his feet and wrapped them too, around the pipe. He carefully climbed horizontally along the pipe, trying to be as quiet as he could. Grime and dust had settled on the top of the pipes and had congealed into a slippery mess, making it hard to grip. He wouldn't have been able to hold on much longer when he eventually made it to where he presumed the private bathroom was.

He found a strong part of the ceiling on which to place his feet and slowly lowered his weight on to it. When he found it able to bear his weight he wasted no time on lifting one of the panels. Below him he saw a clean, modern bathroom. Lowering himself through the hole in the ceiling of the bathroom, he felt around for the sink to rest his foot on. With both feet now on the rim of the sink, he closed over the panel from where he had come and stepped down on to the tiled floor. So far, so good.

Now he could wait for the best time to strike. Hopefully all four would meet again like last week – but he was not sure if it was a regular meeting. If not, Bell would have to do – the rest would either flee the country or he would get them at home. He had seen where they all lived and between him and George they would not pose much of a problem.

He checked his watch – he had made very good time. They still had a couple of hours left of their shift. Cam had really thought it would have taken much longer to get that far, but there he was, in Bell's office and ready to go. It's just a matter of time now.

* * * * * *

Cam sat listening, the time passing slowly. All he could hear was Bell continuing his administrative duties. Cam wondered if it was Torness business or something more sinister. The lights in the en suite bathroom were still off, and the door was ajar by only a few inches. This gave Cam the advantage of being able to hear everything but still remain undetected.

He only hoped that Bell would not need to use his private bathroom, if he did Cam would be exposed and would be forced into taking early action – his mission would only be partly successful. It was now fast approaching one in the morning – not long before their shift would be over. Cam was now concerned that what he witnessed last week was not a regular event. If this was the case, he would have to settle with only Bell. Then between him and George they would have to systematically hunt down the rest of them. This would not be ideal as it would be messy – he would prefer to get it done in one go.

Cam started to remove his rucksack; he only needed his pistol from now on. Remaining in a crouched position, he set down his pack and leant it against the toilet. He then returned to his previous position by the door. He sat against the wall, still listening.

Cam could feel his plan slipping away; he was running out of time. It was fast becoming time to take out Bell, get out of the station, call George, arrange a pick up and start what would become a long night. With one last glance at his watch he stood up and prepared to start the first part of his task. It was now half past one.

The meeting was not happening.

Cam placed his feet shoulder width apart, left foot forward, a classic shooting stance. Still hid behind the partially closed door, he raised his pistol as high as the closed door would allow. With his left hand on the edge of the door he focused all his attention at the area where Bell was sitting at his desk. He visualised the man through the wood of the door – he could see in his mind the man, unaware that he was about to die.

'OK, on the count of three,' he thought. One. He shifted his position slightly into a more comfortable stance. Two. A feeling of nervousness washed over him, this was it. Three!

Knock, knock, knock. Cam froze. That was definitely the sound of someone knocking on the glass of the office door. Next came the sound of a chair leg scraping along the floor, then footsteps.

'Ah Doug, come in.' The office door closed with a clatter. 'Drink?'

'No.'

'Doug, I've been thinking about our um, situation. Phil's little problem is going to make things very difficult for us. We have to decide on a course of action.' Cam stood as still as a rock.

'The plain fact of the matter is that we can no longer trust him.' Cam realised this was the visitor; this was Doug Roberts. 'Should I do it now? I could take them both down,' Cam thought.

'I suggest,' Doug continued, 'that we get rid of Reilly and concentrate on Palmer.'

'Mmm, I agree,' said Bell. 'Take care of it; prepare Palmer for the next one.'

'Good, consider it done.'

'And Doug, I want it done soon.'

Cam knew he should be doing something, but instead he remained where he was, his hand still on the door. He thought there might be still more information he could get from this conversation. But this hope was dashed when he heard the door to the office closing again. 'Damn it.' Cam knew he had missed his chance. He listened as Bell walked across his office floor. He had walked to the other side of the room. The clink of ice cubes falling into a glass was unmistakable. Bell was pouring himself a drink.

'His back must be towards me.' Cam tried to picture the office layout he had seen from the roofing crawl space. 'Let's do this thing!'

Cam increased his grip on the edge of the door and pulled it towards him. As his eyes adjusted to the light of the office, he levelled his pistol at the figure a few metres in front of him. Bell spun round and saw the assassin in the doorway. The only thing Bell could do was throw the glass at his assailant. The ice-filled glass struck Cam on the side of his forehead. The makeshift weapon bounced off the wall and shattered on the floor as Bell launched himself at Cam, rugby tackling him to the floor.

The broken glass crunched underneath the two men as both fought for the advantage. Bell was strong but not strong enough and Cam managed to fight his way on top of him. Cam had him pinned to the floor and forced the barrel of his silencer into the temple of Bell's head. He groaned as the pistol pressed harder and harder into the side of his head. Cam began to take up the pressure of the trigger, Bell was only a few pounds per square inch away from death.

'Rich, what the hell was …?' Cam looked up at the open office door. Doug Roberts stood still, taking in the scene before him; he was in shock. Cam shifted his aim towards his new target.

'In,' he said. Doug did not move. 'Get inside!' Cam said more forcefully.

'Do as he says, Doug,' said Bell.

He did as he was told, still staring at what was happening.

'Shut the door.'

He followed the order and then, in what seemed to be an act of blind panic, lunged towards the large wooden desk that Bell had been working at. Thump, Thump, Thump! Cam let off a series of well-aimed shots as the man dived across the room.

'Argghh!' screamed Roberts as he crumpled to the floor behind the desk. Cam raised his right hand and with all his might brought the pistol grip down on the back of Bell's head. He was out cold. Cam next walked over to the desk to reveal an injured man frantically pressing a hidden button under the desk. 'Shit! A panic alarm.'

Thump, thump. Two more shots ripped into Roberts' thighs and he screamed in agony. Cam grabbed a roll of tape from the desk and began wrapping it round Roberts' mouth, muffling his cries. He then dragged him by the hair over to the unconscious Bell. Pulling some zip ties from his trouser pockets he began tying their hands behind their backs.

It was only now he felt the pain on the side of his head. With the back of his pistol hand he felt the wound. When he brought his hand away he saw the blood – not much, but he could have done without this. Feeling anger to be in this situation he leaned over and slapped Bell about the face until he came round. He looked up, squinting with the pain in the back of his head.

'What does that button do?' The two men sat in silence. 'Well?' Still nothing. 'OK, here's what's going to happen. You're going to tell me what you guys have planned for your two brainwashed morons down there. Or you are going to die, right here, right now.' He looked at the two men, then when there was no response he levelled his pistol between Roberts' eyes. 'You have ten seconds.'

'Don't move!' A shout rang out almost immediately after the door was kicked in, with such force it slammed against the wall, shattering the glass. In the doorway stood a police officer, armed and aiming at Cam.

'Sir,' said Cam, as he slowly raised his arms. He had no choice but to enlist the help of the CNC officer. 'I am a government agent; I am here because we have reason to believe these two men are involved in terrorist activities. There are two more and I could use your help in apprehending them.'

'Do you have any ID?' replied the officer.

'No.'

'Do you have any proof?'

'Nothing I could show you.'

'How can I believe you?'

'You probably shouldn't – however, they are behind the failed attack on St James' shopping centre and are planning something else similar. You have a real chance to make a difference to national security here.'

There was a long silence – a very long silence.

'OK, what's happened and what do we need to do?' The police officer lowered his weapon and approached Cam.

'We've had these two under surveillance for some time now and there are two more: Phil Reilly and Steve Palmer. I could use them both up here. Can you organise that?'

'Yeah, no problem. Is he all right?' The police officer pointed at Roberts.

'He'll be fine,' lied Cam.

As Cam looked down at Roberts, he felt a huge weight smash down on the back of his neck. He fell to the ground; his vision blurred and fizzed like an old black-and-white television. From his hands and knees he shook his head trying to gain back some control. 'What the hell was that?' he thought as he looked up to see the fist of the police officer inches away from his face.

Chapter 27

'Good work, James, get me out of these.'

Cam groaned and rolled around on the floor. He drifted in and out of consciousness.

'Who the hell is this guy?... There must be more of them!... Calm down, we're still in control!... Get everyone up here! Go! ... What about him?... Next door, tie him up.'

Cam woke; he was handcuffed behind his back and sat on some kind of desk chair.

'He's awake, Sir.'

Looking around through a splitting headache, Cam saw all four of his targets – plus the one new one. Roberts was slumped in the corner of the room, which was an abandoned office. He didn't look too good, there was a lot of blood pooling around him and he looked grey and lifeless.

'James, go to work on this guy. When we get back I will want answers out of him.' On that, three of the men left.

Only the new individual and the now probably dead Roberts remained.

'Well, well, well. We are gonna have some fun now,' said James. Whack. He punched Cam hard in the face. Whack – again and again. Cam's head buzzed. He spat out some blood as his attacker lifted his foot and slammed it into Cam's chest, sending the wheeled chair skidding across the room and colliding against the wall. Cam's head bashed against the bricks. Again and again, James rained down punches on the helpless Cam. He had no idea how much more he could take. Then, just before he could bear no more, the assault stopped and he lowered his face to the bloody mess of Cam's head.

'You wait here, I've got an idea.' With that he opened the door, saying, 'I'll be back in a minute.'

Alone in the room, apart from Roberts' lifeless body, he struggled to stay conscious. He resisted the urge to drift into the pleasant place where your body refuses to know or acknowledge what's happening to it. His eyes stung with sweat and blood as he sought a way out of his predicament. It hurt to raise his head, but he had no choice, he had no idea how long he had before James got back.

The new room he found himself in appeared to be unoccupied – they must have moved him while he was unconscious, it still, however, had the left-over furniture and stationery of the previous occupant. Cam rolled his chair backwards over to the cluttered desk, crashing into it and further rattling his head. Gritting his teeth and clenching his stomach muscles, he leaned forward, trying to lift his weight out of the chair. After a few attempts he managed to get to his feet. The chair he was handcuffed to dangled from his wrists as he felt around behind his back to as much of the table as he could reach.

He found a pen and removed the lid. He examined it with his fingers. 'That'll do.' He collapsed back on the chair. He bent back the metal clip of the lid, back and forward, back and forward until it snapped from the lid, which he dropped to the floor. He tried to feel the handcuffs that held his hands behind his back. With the pen-lid clip in between the finger and thumb of his right hand, he found the teeth and locking mechanism that was tight around his wrist. If he had been awake when they were placed he would have forced his wrists towards the person applying them. That way they would have been tightened around his forearms rather than his wrists, giving more room to play with – but he didn't have that luxury.

He inserted the flat metal shim between the teeth and the locking mechanism; the handcuffs slid open. Now free, Cam leaned forward and fell to the floor. He propped himself up against the wooden desk leg and removed his other wrist from the cuffs. Cam sat and tried to collect his thoughts; he had to resist the urge to wipe the blood from his face and out of his eyes. He had to look the same as when James left.

* * * * * * *

'You look pathetic,' James said, as he walked back into the room. Cam hoped he wouldn't see any change in his posture. With blood still covering his face, he burbled a few incomprehensible words.

'I've got a treat for you,' he said as he flicked open an extendable metal police baton. 'They're going to be back in a minute, but before that, I'm going to break every bone in your body.' The man sounded like he was enjoying himself just a little too much. 'This,' he said as he lifted Cam's chin with the baton, 'is what we call the bone-cruncher.'

Cam slowly opened his eyes to look directly into the face of his new enemy. The two men made eye contact and Cam could tell the man was a true psychopath; he seemed to be relishing in the brutality of the situation.

James straightened up and drew in a breath with closed eyes. It seemed to Cam that he was getting a thrill from this. He looked down and raised his baton – but before he had a chance to inflict any more injuries, Cam lifted his foot and sent it crashing into James' knee. Cam heard the sound of bone cracking, followed by a loud scream as James fell to the ground in agony. Cam stood up, free from his shackles, and stood down hard on James' wrist, securing his weapon to the ground. As he bent down to take the baton from his hand he saw the injury to his knee, it was bent forward at a very unnatural angle.

'That looks sore,' he whispered into his ear.

Now Cam was in control – but he was still short of time. James writhed around on the floor as the baton smashed into the back of his skull. Confident he had inflicted a fatal blow, Cam stepped away from the shaking body. He walked backwards to where Roberts' grey body laid slumped in the corner. Checking his pulse he confirmed he was dead – he had bled out where he was left. Returning his focus to the officer, he saw that he was in the final death throes, shaking outstretched on the floor, head and back arched, his arms by his sides, fists clenched and extending away from his body. 'Decerebrate posturing – that's about it for him,' Cam thought as he placed the baton in Doug Roberts' lifeless hand.

Now he had to find the other three. Not knowing where his own pistol was, he would have to make do with the one James had hit him over the head with. He found it still in his holster; he pulled it out and also took the spare magazine. The police officer had stopped shaking. He opened the door and looked down the corridor. From his position he saw he had been moved to the office next to Bell's. Listening hard for the others he heard nothing.

The whole place seemed to be deserted. He had more time than he had expected. He ducked back into the room with the bodies. Cam went into the en suite bathroom of the deserted office, picked up a small face-cloth and began to clean himself up. The warm water stung his wounds as he washed his face in the sink. Once he was as clean as he could get himself, he looked into the mirror at his bruised and battered face.

'I look like shit,' he said, as he cracked his neck off to one side. He wiped up the sink to leave as little trace as possible that he was there, then stuffed the face cloth into his pocket.

* * * * * * *

Leaning with both hands on the edge of the sink he heard the sound of someone walking over broken glass. 'That's Bell's office,' he thought. He immediately left the bathroom. Back at the door he again had a good look both ways down the corridor. There was definite movement in Bell's office. Cam quietly shut the door, hiding the bodies, and silently crept to the smashed glass door of Bell's office.

Wanting to keep the element of surprise, he was not going to peek through into the room – the last thing he wanted was to be spotted. He was just going to have to go for it; hopefully they would not be expecting anything. As far as they knew he was being beaten next door.

'You, over there!' He motioned for one of the men whom he recognised as Palmer to move over to the two-seat sofa in the corner of the room. He had caught the two men by surprise. 'You, still!' He ordered Bell not to move as he approached Palmer. Both men had their hands in the air as Cam picked up one of the sofa cushions; he pushed it into Palmer's face. He raised the police officer's Glock pistol. A muffled bang threw Palmer against the far wall and he slid down dead to the floor. A cloud of feathers fluttered down and covered the body. Cam turned his attention to Bell – who was now looking terrified. He had him exactly how he wanted him; ready to talk.

'Where's Reilly?'

Bell's eyes darted around the room, looking for any way out of this situation. 'Look at me.' Cam said calmly. 'I'll ask you again. Where is Reilly?' Bell remained silent. Cam stepped up to him and jammed the pistol into the side of his head. Bell closed his eyes and dropped his arms slightly in an attempt to protect his head. 'Where is Reilly?' Cam demanded.

'On his way to reactor control room one.' The fast response was almost automatic. Bell had not wanted to say anything; it was simply a natural self-defence response.

'Why?'

Bell thought for a second. 'You're too late. In a few minutes half of Scotland and the North of England will be uninhabitable. You fucked my plans up; I'm gonna fuck you up.'

Those were Bell's last words. The bullet ripped through his head and he went limp and fell to the floor.

In a second Cam was up and running. He grabbed his rucksack that he spotted lying on a table in the office and swung it on his back as he moved. He had no time at all. Corridor after corridor he bashed his way through doors, trying to get back outside. As he moved he fished in his pocket for his phone, he found it and quickly tapped in his code. The map of Torness appeared on the screen. He had left the document open in case he needed to check it. As he ran out into the fresh air he slid into his ear the Bluetooth earpiece Al had given him.

'Give me a sit rep,' said Al.

'Targets eliminated except one. Reilly is about to destroy reactor one. I'm en route now.'

'We have you on screen now; do you know where you're going?'

'I have a map on the phone, should be there in a few minutes.'

'Put your phone away. I'll relay directions in real time, you prep yourself, OK?'

'Yeah, OK,' panted Cam. He was starting to tire.

'Left, left,' instructed Al. Cam bore left, pushing himself to go faster and faster. The nuclear power station had only on a skeleton crew at that time of night. All he had to do was make sure he didn't run into any police patrols.

He knew he was running past many cameras, but he had no choice, the station was about to be destroyed and only he could prevent it.

'Go right here, Cam and there's a door about thirty metres ahead.'

'Shit, there's a code, Al, there's a code!' Cam wheezed. He was out of breath.

'Wait, wait.'

Cam waited for what seemed like forever.

'Well! What do I do?'

'4, 7, 2, 7, 2.'

Cam punched in the code and the door bleeped. He opened it.

'Shit, Al, there's people in here!' Cam slipped into the shadows. He looked around the open spaced room. It was about the size of an aircraft hanger and lit with bright neon lights, but there were many dark shadows; the light was blocked by tables, large banks of machinery and structural pillars. Above him there were walkways; Cam could see at least one man up there. This was not good; he would have to stay out of that guy's view.

'How many?' Al asked.

'Three or four,' whispered Cam. 'They're just milling about. I'm moving in.'

Cam sneaked forward, following the walls. He kept to the shadows as he looked up, keeping an eye on his main threat.

'I'm working on something here; it might give you an edge.'

Cam did not reply – he needed to stay quiet. He's in here somewhere. He continued further into the reactor control room. He stayed low and trod quietly. He passed a lone worker checking on some machinery; he was only feet away from him but passed unnoticed. He stopped for a moment to rest the thighs he had been exerting so much as he crept through the shadows.

'Cam, got it! This might help you out.' With that, out went the lights. Cam remained still in the now pitch-black hanger, listening to the commotion that the sudden blackout has caused.

'That's good,' Cam said as he fished out his night vision goggles. 'They're preoccupied. I'm searching for Reilly.'

The hanger lit up in a green and black haze. Cam could see perfectly. The shouting workers were trying frantically to restore the lighting system. They now had torches and he could see the beams of light flashing around. This was good; Cam could keep track of all of them that way. Cam walked around freely – he was almost invisible. He snaked his way left and right between the computer banks, looking for Reilly.

'You have to hurry, this blackout won't last forever.'

'It's a big room, Al,' Cam said quietly, still hunting for his last target.

The green glow of the night vision goggles revealed row after empty row between the tables and cabinets. Cam decided to stop and listen; he turned off his NVGs. That stopped the high-pitched whine but also, without sight, his other senses were heightened. He slowly looked round, trying to detect the very slight sound that he now had picked up. Slowly moving in the direction of the sound, it turned into heavy breathing. He could hear mumbling, like someone talking to themselves.

Cam was now as close as he could be to the sound without giving himself away. Cam flicked on his night vision and with a growing green glow he saw a man crouched in a gap between a set of filing cabinets. After a couple more steps he stopped and levelled his gun at the hunched figure.

'Reilly!' he whispered. With a gasp, Reilly looked up towards the hidden source of the voice.

'Who's there? Is that you, Sir?'

Cam could now see what he was cradling in his arms. It was another suicide vest, similar to the one Brant used in the St James job.

'You're too late, Reilly, it's over. Give me the device.' Reilly hunted frantically for the trigger. 'He's going to do it!' He couldn't shoot; the un-silenced pistol would bring everyone down on him, but there was no way he could allow the device to be detonated.

He stepped forward out of the shadows and into Reilly's view.

'Who are you?' Reilly asked, as he gripped the string toggle that would cause the vest to explode. 'I'll do it! I'll do it!' he growled at Cam.

'No, you won't,' Cam replied as he broke his aim on his target. He placed his weapon in his leg holster and showed his empty hands to the desperate man. 'I'm here to help you; I want to get you out of here and away from Bell and the rest of them.'

Reilly stared at Cam; sweat began to drip down his face as he looked at the man in black, his face hidden by goggles.

'I have to, I have no choice!' He said as he took up the slack on the string.

'No, no! Wait, wait, wait,' pleaded Cam. 'Look, I know all about you. I know about your problems. You don't want to be here, doing this. You need help to escape. I can help you.' Reilly seemed to relax his grip. 'Give me the device, and let's get out of here. Come on.' Cam beckoned, indicating that he wanted the vest. 'Give it here.'

Reilly stood up, his legs shaking visibly. He looked at the vest then at Cam.

'Good man,' Cam said as he took the vest from the defeated-looking man.

'Well done, Cam,' said Al. He had followed the tense verbal exchange.

'What now?' Reilly said, still staring at Cam.

'What do you want done with him, Al?'

Reilly looked quizzically at Cam, who continued to await instructions. Reilly shifted uncomfortably as he and Cam stared at each other in silence.

'What do I do now?' Reilly repeated.

'Let him go.' Al broke the silence. 'We will track him from here. Get out of there, Cam – but make sure he goes straight home.'

Cam closed in on Reilly, who had not heard what Al had said.

'Listen to me very carefully. Get yourself home. Go nowhere else. Somebody will be in contact. Do you understand me?'

'Yes, I understand.'

'Go. Now!' Reilly hurried off into the darkness. Cam breathed a sigh of relief, but knew he was not in the clear yet. He had to get out himself.

Chapter 28

Cam picked his way back to the area of fence that he cut on his way in. All the time Al watched via satellite and helped him avoid patrols and the odd wandering worker.

'This helps Al. Why can't we do this all the time?' Cam asked.

'I think we will from now on – if it's required that is. I'll organise better communication for us though.'

'OK, Al,' Cam said as he reached the small shack, just in view of the fence.

'Here's the situation. You know about Reilly – the others are all dead. There was one more – a man called James.'

'James! Who the hell is James?'

'He was a CNC police officer.'

'Christ! And he was one of them?'

'Yes, he will be found dead in the office next to Bell's, battered to death with his own extendable baton. That baton will be found in the hand of Doug Roberts, who died in the same office, shot with my silenced P226. I lost my pistol, took James' Glock and shot Bell and Palmer dead in Bell's office. I have all my own equipment except my P226. No other traces of me apart from a cut fence and probably some appearances on CCTV.'

'Bloody hell! Anything else?'

'No, that's about it.'

'OK, I'll come up with some sort of cover story. I'm going to send George round to Reilly's and see what information he can get from him. Hopefully you got everyone. Get out and back home, I'll be in contact.'

'OK, no problem. Is the coast clear?'

'Yes, no patrols anywhere near you. I think they are all busy with the black-out and some unexplained CCTV images.'

Cam dashed for the fence, cut his own zip ties, crawled out and used more ties to repair the cuts. As he ran away from the power station he felt an overwhelming sense of relief, and as he ran the adrenaline started to wear off. The familiar feeling of fatigue that always followed operations like that started to drain his body of energy.

George's car came into view parked in a lay-by. Cam opened the rear door of the car and threw his rucksack on to the seat; he then carefully placed the device on the floor of the car. Cam climbed into the passenger seat next to George who looked over and started laughing.

'What the hell happened to you? You look like shit!'

'Long, long story mate,' he said.

'Well, it's a long drive.'

George laughed as Cam went over the whole story. The cuts and bruises on Cam's face start to ache and sting as he recounted the night's events.

'You've had quite a night – but you did well. We're both still here and so is the north of the country – so good work.'

Cam pulled down the sun visor and looked into the passenger mirror.

'God almighty, look at that,' he said, surveying the wounds on his face.

'Yep, you're gonna have a few bruises in the morning. So what about Reilly?'

'Oh yeah, Al's going to be sending you round there to get info out of him.'

'Good, it will be a pleasure,' said George, smiling.

Cam stumbled wearily into his flat. He was exhausted, both physically and mentally. He found just enough strength to put his equipment away, and opened his hidden weapon cupboard and placed each piece of equipment in its place. James' Glock replaced his own silenced P226 and he made a mental note to ask for a new one next time he spoke to Al.

He cleaned the cuts, not only on his face, but new ones that he found all over his body, and stepped into the shower. His face stung as the warm water rushed over him, waking him up a little bit. He dried himself off and put on a pair of shorts and a t-shirt. His apartment was uncomfortably warm.

He poured himself a large Bells whisky, and as he did so, laughed at the name. 'Bells, Christ!' He stood at his window and gazed out over the city that he has saved for a second time. But nobody would ever know. After finishing off his whisky he slumped on to the sofa and immediately fell asleep.

* * * * * * *

Cam spent the next few days watching the news channels. One story dominated the headlines. A murder had been committed at Torness Nuclear Power Station –apparently by a member of the Civil Nuclear Constabulary. As the full story came out, it conspired that the police officer had shot and killed three people in the main office building. A hero had emerged through the tragedy; a man called Doug Roberts had managed to stop the police officer by overpowering him and attacking him with his own police baton. Unfortunately, he died from a gun-shot wound to the stomach. 'Doug Roberts!' Cam thought to himself. 'A hero!' If only they knew the real story. But they never would.

The days began to pass by and Cam was slipping back into his comfortable life. After cleaning and tidying away his equipment, he locked up his weapons cupboard and promised to forget it was even there until the next job. He hoped he might get some time to himself, to rest. A few days later Cam returned from his daily run and was standing in the kitchen leaning on the breakfast bar when he heard his phone ringing.

'Cam, its George, how's the face?'

'Good mate, getting better, how did it go with Reilly?'

'We had an interesting conversation. Have you heard from Al?'

'No, why?'

'No reason. Hey check out *The Edinburgh Evening News*. Speak to you later.' With that George abruptly ended the conversation and Cam decided to go for another run.

He ran down the street to his closest newsagent where he bought a copy of the local newspaper. Still sweating from his run, he stood in the street, flicking through the paper. He had no idea what he was looking for until he turned to page seven. There at the bottom of the page, barely noticeable, was a small article. Skimming the paragraph Cam read about the suicide of Phil Reilly. The poor drug-addicted petty criminal had hanged himself in his house. Cam lowered the newspaper and wondered what really happened. Did he kill himself – or did George and Al have something to do with it? Whatever had happened, Reilly was out of the way and would not be able to reveal the truth.

Paper in hand, Cam made his way back to his flat for a shower. As he stood under the water, he kept looking over at his phone that he had placed on the side of the sink. He dressed and started to prepare his dinner, occasionally glancing over at the still silent phone. 'When are you going to ring?' he thought. He was desperate to know what had happened and what Al wanted.

Then it happened – it finally rang.

'Hello,' Cam said.

'Cam, it's Al.'

'Hello, Al.'

'Have you seen the story?'

'Yeah, how much did you have to do with that?'

'Me, nothing – but George got some rather interesting information out of him before he, er, killed himself.'

'Oh yeah. What was that then?'

'Take a seat, this might take a while. Firstly, George found out that this guy James was James Green, CNC Police Officer. He was part of the cell and a bit of a psycho, but I think you found that out for yourself.'

'I certainly did,' Cam replied, stretching his jaw from side to side.

'Hey, what did you think of my cover story?'

'Yeah, good one. Fits well.'

'Thanks. Anyway, George confirmed that the whole team has been eliminated. Well done.'

'So that's it – we're done?'

'Not quite. We found out how Bell was recruiting his team,' Al continued. 'Reilly was befriended in prison by the same man who shared a cell with Palmer. This is the man who is converting the weak-minded first-timers. He's the last piece of the puzzle, and I have arranged to get him paroled from prison. It's going to take a couple of weeks, but I'll get him out – then he'll be an easy target.' Al paused. 'This man is the only remaining piece in this whole mess. How would you feel about having a tidy up?'

Chapter 29

The night was dark, warm but cloudy. The moon occasionally broke through, bathing the sleeping city in silver light. The man was fast asleep, enjoying his new freedom. He had been kept in solitary confinement before his release. He hadn't even been able to watch television or listen to the radio – but that had just made his release all the sweeter. Tomorrow he would meet his old friend Richard Bell.

'What was that?' He woke with a start and sat bolt upright. Had he heard something? Or was he just not used to the silence of freedom. No – something was wrong. He climbed out of bed and slowly moved towards the bedroom door. He was still unsure of the layout of his new house, but he didn't want to turn on the lights – he was too freaked out about what he might find.

'Hello,' he whispered. 'Is anyone there?' He peeked out of his bedroom and down the corridor. He saw nothing but moonlight through a break in the clouds casting long shadows down the hallway. Then he heard it again. What was that? It could be something flapping in the breeze. It seemed to be coming from outside. He let out a sigh of relief and stepped out into the corridor.

As he came to the top of the stairs he stopped. The hair on the back of his neck stood up and a shiver went down his back. Something was behind him. He turned slowly to face the open doorway to the second bedroom. He shuffled over to the dark opening. Without going through the door, he tried to peer in. The low light in the corridor wouldn't allow his night vision to adjust to the pitch-black room.

As he leaned forward, a black-gloved hand shot out of the darkness, grabbing his neck. He let out a shriek as he was pulled into the room and thrown to the floor. He spun round on the floor in a desperate attempt to see who or what had attacked him. He could see nothing as he crawled away from the doorway. Then out of the darkness emerged a figure.

Barely visible in the gloom, the figure was dressed in black; only his eyes could be seen, staring at him through a balaclava.

'What do you want?' he demanded, as the dark figure raised a gun in his direction. 'No, no, wait.' The intruder didn't reply, or even move. 'How did you get in here?' He tried to again to get a response. Then, after a long silence, the man replied.

'I can get in anywhere.'

He knew from the glare in his assailant's eyes that he was about to die. He could see him taking up the slack on the trigger. It was about to happen.

'Who the hell are you?'

'I am Sterling!'

Sterling Returns

in

Assets

Two years after the Torness job Cam is sent on his next deadly assignment. A rouge Iranian General has disappeared with an arsenal of deadly chemical weapons and is threatening to unleash them on his countries enemies.

Joined by old friends and new, Cam must hunt down and find this dangerous man before he holds to ransom the counties of the Gulf of Oman and the surrounding states.

Join the Assets on their first international adventure, from civilised Dubai to unstable Yemen. Follow as Cam and his team close in on the enemy.

Can the Assets locate the missing weapons in time?

Coming Autumn 2013